BITTER HARVEST

When she learns that her partner is not only unfaithful, but is also a confidence trickster, Michaela Clarke believes that she can never trust a man again. While struggling to come to terms with what has happened to her she meets handsome Jerome Marshall. While instantly attracted to him, she is wary of becoming involved again, especially as he comes from an enormously wealthy family. Can love find a way?

Books by Catriona McCuaig
in the Linford Romance Library:

CATRIONA McCUAIG

BITTER
HARVEST

Complete and Unabridged

LINFORD
Leicester

First published in Great Britain in 2007

First Linford Edition
published 2008

British Library CIP Data

McCuaig, Catriona
    Bitter harvest.—Large print ed.—
Linford romance library
1. Love stories
2. Large type books
I. Title
823.9′2 [F]

ISBN 978–1–84782–184–3

Published by
F. A. Thorpe (Publishing)
Anstey, Leicestershire

Set by Words & Graphics Ltd.
Anstey, Leicestershire
Printed and bound in Great Britain by
T. J. International Ltd., Padstow, Cornwall

This book is printed on acid-free paper

1

All in the space of a week, Lady Frances Carew had experienced love, intrigue and the discovery of a murder, although not necessarily in that order. She had, of course, emerged victorious on all counts. Michaela Clarke closed the book with a sigh. She really must stop immersing herself in Gothic novels and concentrate on real life.

She had everything to be grateful for. A job she enjoyed, a pleasant flat and, most important of all, a fiancé she adored. Tom Bowman might not be Brad Pitt, but he was extremely attractive in his own way, with his piercing blue eyes and lopsided grin.

He was very much an outdoor man, with sandy hair bleached by the sun and a tan which seemed to last all year, the product of his work as a golf pro at an exclusive club. She and Tom had been together for the past six months and planned to marry when the time seemed right.

The problem now was that she was feeling bored. Tom was working late again and she couldn't think of anything she felt like doing on her own. She leapt to her feet when the door bell rang. Tom's evening appointment must have been cancelled and here he was, having forgotten his key as usual.

'Hello, Mickey! I thought I'd pop round and see if you wanted to do something this evening. I'm not interrupting anything, am I?'

'Come in, Sandie.' Mickey stood aside to let her friend pass. 'Actually when the door bell went I thought it might be Tom, getting home early for once.'

'Oh.' Sandie looked uncomfortable and Mickey realised she must have sounded less than gracious. She hastened to put things right. 'I'm so glad you came, Sandie. I was feeling at a loose end. Were you thinking of getting in a video or something?'

'On a lovely June evening like this? No way! I thought we'd go for a walk in the park, or even rent a row boat and whittle down our waistlines. What do you think?'

Mickey's eyes opened wide as an idea struck her. 'I tell you what would be even better. Let's walk up to the golf course and we can watch Tom from the clubhouse where he can't spot us. He's giving some extra lessons to a new member, which is why he isn't home just now. I did suggest going with him, but he said it would put him off his stroke if he knew I was there, looking on.'

'Oh, I don't know,' Sandie objected. 'Don't you think it might upset him?'

'Upset him? What on earth are you talking about? It can't do any harm if he doesn't know we're there.'

Sandie bit her lip. 'Somebody might let it slip later.' Mickey was looking at her curiously so she improvised swiftly. 'I mean, he is the pro at the club. That's how he earns his living. The committee might not like him taking his fiancée to work, so to speak.'

Mickey raised her eyebrows. 'You worry too much. It's not like us taking friends to the office where we work, you know. Outsiders are welcome at the club as the guests of members. Why, you went there last week with that Brendan Powell you've been seeing. I know you did.'

That was just the problem. Sandie had been to the club, and she'd seen Tom Bowman who was all over a girl who certainly wasn't Mickey. Of course giving golf lessons was part of his job, but that didn't involve walking back to the club house hand in hand with one of his pupils, or kissing her forehead as they paused at the door to the restaurant. Sandie had also seen them together in the town. Tom was up to no good and she had spent some sleepless nights wondering whether to tell Mickey about it.

'Oh, well, if you really want to go to

4

the club . . . ' she began. Perhaps it was just as well to let Mickey see for herself. She'd have to know sometime and this way Sandie wouldn't have to be the informer.

'No, no. Not if it makes you that uncomfortable,' Mickey responded. 'Why don't we go to the park and see if there's a tennis court free?'

The next time she saw Brendan, Sandie decided to pump him for information.

'Who is that new woman at the golf club, the one with all that long auburn hair?'

'Oh, you mean Felicity! Isn't she gorgeous? Rolling in money, too, I'm told!'

'Why, what does she do for a living?'

'Nothing, as far as I know. She's one of life's butterflies, there for ornamental purposes only! It's Daddy's money. He owns a string of factories somewhere in the north. I don't know what he manufactures.'

Sandie wasn't interested in that.

'What's she doing here, then?'

He shrugged. 'Staying with her aunt and uncle, I believe. You know, old Smythe on the committee.'

'So that's why she's taking lessons? She wants to improve her game.'

Brendan sniggered. 'I know what her game is, all right, and our Tom is playing right along. I'd say he's fairly well smitten.'

Sandie said nothing in response to this and he looked at her in some concern. 'I say, isn't he supposed to be engaged to that friend of yours, Mickey somebody? I'm sorry if I spoke out of turn. I didn't think.'

'It's OK, Brendan. You only put into words what I already suspected. My problem now is whether to let Mickey know what's been going on behind her back.'

'I wish I hadn't said anything now!' Brendan sounded alarmed. 'It's probably just a bit of innocent flirtation, Sandie. It goes with the territory, see? Keep the punters happy and all that.'

'I hope that's all it is,' she murmured.

'Then you won't say anything, eh? What's the point of getting everybody all worked up? And if Tom and Felicity are having a bit of a whirl it'll play itself out all in good time and your Mickey will be none the wiser.'

'You men like to stick together, don't you,' Sandie observed sourly, but Brendan didn't rise to the bait.

Meanwhile, Mickey was becoming annoyed with Tom. He seemed to be working day and night. She began to wonder what the point in seeing someone if she got little out of the relationship. Was this what being married to him was going to be like?

'I'm a bit worried about you working so hard,' she said at last, but he simply said he wouldn't be doing it forever, and that things would settle down when winter came.

'I want to make as much money as I can, while I can,' he explained. 'Surely you can understand that if you want that holiday in Australia, we have to save as much as possible.'

Mickey's parents were currently living in Canberra where her father was on a job exchange. Mickey had opted to stay behind, partly because she didn't want to leave Tom, even for a short time, and partly because she liked her job at the insurance agency and didn't want to lose seniority there.

The holiday in Australia had been Tom's idea. He had always wanted to see that country and it wouldn't cost much over and above their fares because they'd be able to stay with her parents.

As a result they'd opened a joint savings account and were saving hard. At least, Mickey was. She had just made a deposit and when the passbook was updated she was dismayed to see that Tom didn't seem to have put in much of anything, and nothing at all for some weeks. So what was he doing with all that overtime money?

She was puzzled by the look in Sandie's eyes during their lunch hour from work when she had a little moan about this, and then felt compelled to come to Tom's defence.

'I expect he's put his whole pay cheque into his regular account and forgotten to transfer funds into our holiday fund. I'll have to remind him.'

'What will you do if you save enough for your fare but he doesn't?' Sandie wondered. 'I hope you won't think of paying his way as well! Not when your parents have offered you what amounts to board and lodgings while you're in Australia.'

Mickey laughed. 'I doubt it! After we're married, of course, things will be different, we'll share everything then. In the meantime, I don't think Tom would appreciate being a kept man.'

Sandie laughed obediently, but her heart wasn't in it. There were plenty of things she wanted to say, but she held her tongue.

'Tom's going away this weekend to play in a tournament,' Mickey said now.

'And you're going too, are you?'

'I don't think so. He hasn't said anything to that effect and I don't want to pressure him. I mean, we're not joined at the hip or anything, are we? He deserves a bit of time to himself.'

'You're engaged, for heaven's sake! If I were you I'd pack a bag and follow him out the door when he leaves. As I see it you've been home alone far too much lately, and the pair of you need some quality time together.'

But Mickey seemed disinclined to discuss it further and Sandie went back to her cubicle feeling saddened. Her friend was far too trusting, and she was convinced that it could only end in tears.

2

The girls were staring a little enviously at their supervisor, Mrs Phipps. She had just finished telling them that a distant cousin was getting married in Spain, and she'd received an invitation. Remarkably, she was in two minds about going.

'My husband's not all that keen,' she explained. 'It's all to do with the food, you see. I'm afraid he's one of those people who can't abide what he likes to call 'foreign muck' and he's utterly miserable without his meat and two veg. I don't fancy going on my own, and if I force him to go I'll never hear the end of it. No, I think I'll just send them a wedding gift and tell them we can't get away.'

'If I'm ever invited to a family gathering in a foreign country I'll go like a shot,' Sandie smiled. 'Wouldn't you like to travel the world?'

'Certainly I would, and Australia is first on my list!' Mickey said firmly. 'I must say I'd like to see Spain, though. Perhaps in the future . . . '

'If you mean to get married and have three children and a dog,' Sandie laughed, 'you'll be too tied down to travel until you're old and grey!'

Mickey didn't answer. She seemed to be staring off into the middle distance. Tom didn't seem as interested in discussing future plans as he once had, and she couldn't quite understand this. Wasn't it natural to talk about the size of their future family? More than that, it was only sensible to do so before the wedding took place, in case each partner had a different view of things.

The question of income was also an important issue. At present their joint wage packets kept them going quite nicely, but what would happen if Tom became the sole wage earner? He had once said that he wouldn't want his wife going out to work when the children came along. Their mother should stay at home to give them a good start in life. That was all very well, but suppose they had a mortgage to keep up? Their tiny flat was fine for two working people, but not big enough for a family.

'What's on your mind, Mickey?'

'What? Oh!' She came to with a start. 'I'm just wondering how Tom is getting along at the tournament, that's all.'

'You haven't heard from him, then?'

'No. I tried him a couple of times, but his mobile is switched off.'

'That's odd, isn't it?'

'Not really. He wouldn't be popular if it rang just when someone was lining up a marvellous shot and it put them off. I'll call later this evening.'

'Oh, I expect he'll call you if he wins,' Sandie murmured, although she had her own thoughts as to where Tom was and why he was incommunicado. 'How do you think he'll do in the competition?'

'Hard to say.' Mickey didn't want to

seem disloyal, but she doubted if Tom stood a chance among the expert players who would be there. As someone who had golfed since he was a young boy, it had been his dream to turn professional, competing for big prizes among the best in the world but, sadly, he didn't have the talent. He was a clever, reliable player who fell just short of the standard required.

He was the perfect example of the old adage, *Those who can, do. Those who can't, teach*. He earned a reasonable salary at the golf club, but would rise no higher than that.

It seemed obvious to Mickey that the time was fast approaching when he would have to seek out a different line of work, but she didn't like to say so. That would have been too cruel and she thought it best to wait patiently until he came to the same conclusion. So far that hadn't happened.

Later that day she tried again to reach him, without success. She tried again at nine, and then an hour later, but he still wasn't answering. She concluded that he must have forgotten to switch it on again after the excitement of the day. Probably some of the contestants were celebrating in a pub somewhere, and Tom was with them.

★   ★   ★

'I'm home!' Tom burst through the door, beaming. Mickey threw herself into his arms, delighted to see him.

'It feels like you've been gone forever!' she breathed. 'How did you get on? Did everything go all right?'

'Here, steady on! You'll have me over! Go and put the kettle on, will you? I'm gasping for a cuppa. Just wait till I get my feet up and I'll tell you all about it.'

She did as he asked. 'So come on then, tell me all about it!' she demanded, when he was comfortably ensconced in their one and only armchair, sipping is tea.

'Nothing to tell, really.'

'Don't be silly. Of course there is. Who did you play against?'

If you really must know, I didn't get to play at all. Somebody ran me down with a golf cart and I sprained my ankle.'

'But I thought carts weren't allowed during tournaments? Haven't you told me that before?'

'Well, there was one there, and it knocked me flat, all right.'

Mickey felt most indignant on his behalf, and offered to fetch ice to put on the ankle. He waved her away crossly. 'It's all right now. The St John's people fixed me up. Don't fuss, Mickey!'

Seeing her downcast look he softened his manner and told her to fetch his overnight bag. 'When I couldn't play I left early, and went into the town to buy you a present. Two presents, in fact!' He handed her a silk scarf and a small bottle of eau de toilette.

'It's lovely, Tom! Thank you so much!'

The silk square was indeed lovely, a paisley design in shades of pink, mauve and purple. It wouldn't go with any of her clothes, but that didn't matter.

It was not until much later, when Mickey asked herself where his golf clubs were. Not in the boot of the car, surely. He was meticulous about never leaving anything of value there, even when the car was locked. Nowadays you can't trust anyone, he used to say.

Cars could be stolen, vandalised, even cannibalised the minute your back was turned. When the day came that they could finally afford to move, it would have to be somewhere with an attached garage. She fell asleep, still wondering about the clubs.

The next morning she set off for work in high spirits, taking the silk square with her to show Sandie, carefully wrapped up in tissue paper inside her handbag. Sandie duly admired it, saying that it looked expensive.

Always joking, she blurted out

without thinking that Tom must have been up to something and had bought the presents because he was feeling guilty. She stopped short when she saw her friend's stricken face.

'Oh. Mickey, I'm so sorry! It was a joke, you know me. I didn't mean it! I only said it for a laugh. Don't look like that, please.'

'It's just that things don't quite add up, Sandie. Tom told me he was knocked over by a cart and had to get first aid treatment. As a result he was scratched from the tournament. Yet if he was so badly hurt, how was he able to go looking round the shops for this?'

'I expect he took the car,' Sandie said.

'What, and hobbled in and out of all the shops? And that's not all. He came home without his golf clubs and he wouldn't do that in a million years.'

'I expect he stopped off at the Club and stowed them in his locker there, ready for work this morning.'

'Perhaps.'

Sandie realised she was fighting a losing battle so she was pleased when two clients arrived at once. Secretly she thought she could smell a rat, and probably Mickey did too, or wouldn't she have simply asked him where his clubs were?

When she reached home that evening Sandie went straight to her computer and went online. The well-known golf links where Tom was supposed to have been playing had its own website and she wanted to see if they had posted the news of the event yet.

She scanned it quickly, not interested in the announcement of the winners or the prizes they'd received. She scrolled down until she reached a list of all the participants. It was significant that Tom wasn't mentioned.

She sat back, thinking rapidly. Of course, that might be because he'd been injured and had to duck out at the last minute. He hadn't actually played at all. Now what?

She jotted down the club phone

number and was soon speaking to the secretary.

'I represent *The Courier*,' she fibbed. 'One of our local players was due to take part in your tournament this weekend. Can you tell me how he did? He is popular at our local club and readers will want to know all about it.'

'What is the gentleman's name, Miss?'

'Tom. Tom Bowman.'

There was a pause as the man checked his computer. 'I'm sorry, there must be a mistake,' he told her. 'There was nobody of that name here. Possibly he was at some other venue. I suggest you interview the man himself if you really want to find out.'

Had Sandie been a real reporter she would have bridled at this, but she didn't want her pretence exposed so she simply thanked him and hung up. 'Now what, Miss Marple?' she said aloud.

Unfortunately she had no idea where

to go next. Not only did she have no proof that Tom had never been near the tournament, but she was still reluctant to confront Mickey with her suspicions.

At the very least it might end their friendship which had endured since their days as small girls in their first term at school. At worst it could colour Mickey's future relationship with Tom, which would be quite wrong if he was innocent after all. On the other hand, wouldn't it be just as wrong to let her go ahead and marry the man if he wasn't trustworthy?

While Sandie was dithering, Mickey was tidying up the flat. She picked up his khaki trousers, which were the kind that had several pockets with button down flaps. They could do with a wash, as could the wet towels which festooned the rim of the bathtub, and with a sigh she decided that she might as well do a load of laundry, being home alone with nothing else to do.

Automatically, she opened the pockets and felt inside for any forgotten items which might fall out in the machine or discolour the other garments.

There was nothing there but a crumpled credit card receipt. She glanced at it idly, noting as she did so that it was from the Metropole Hotel, Bournemouth.

Bournemouth ! When had Tom ever been there? She looked at it more closely, seeing the date, realising with a sinking feeling that it referred to this past weekend.

Sandie's first thought, when she answered the phone and heard Mickey's quavering voice, was a feeling of gratitude that her friend knew about Tom's perfidy and there was no need to raise the subject with her.

'I'll be right over,' she stated. 'There's a bus due about now. If I run I may be able to catch it.' She slammed the phone down, snatched up her handbag and hastened out of the flat.

Mickey had the door open before Sandie had time to ring the bell.

Obviously distraught, she started to talk before they were even sitting down.

'I should have known,' she kept saying. 'I should have known when he kept his mobile turned off all weekend. He didn't go to the tournament at all, did he? Run over by a golf cart, indeed! Of all the silly excuses. He must think I'm a real idiot.'

'What's happened exactly?' Sandie ventured, playing for time.

'Take a look at this if you don't believe me!' Mickey thrust the receipt under her friend's nose. 'If he was where he said he was, where he was supposed to be, why did he pay a hotel bill in Bournemouth?'

'I'm so sorry, Mickey. I've have my suspicions for quite some time that Tom has been two-timing you, but I didn't want to say anything in case I was wrong.'

'Who is she?' Mickey demanded. 'I'll kill him, I absolutely will!' Her face turned pale as the truth sank in. 'How could he do this to me, Sandie? We're saving up to visit my parents in Australia! We're supposed to be getting married for heaven's sake!'

'Perhaps he's having a last fling before settling down,' Sandie suggested, knowing as she said it she would never continue a relationship with a man who did that to her. 'Perhaps you should hear what he has to say before you do anything drastic.'

'Drastic! He lied to me, Sandie. He's been lying through his teeth for weeks.'

Sandie took a deep breath and blurted out everything she knew. It was not a pretty story. As one ugly fact after another came to light Mickey knew without a doubt that her lovely, romantic dream of a life with the man she loved was over, and there was no going back.

3

Somewhere a door slammed, and Mickey's heart leapt, but whoever it was marched past the door of her flat and she knew for the twentieth time that it wasn't Tom, coming to beg her forgiveness, and saying it had all been a horrible mistake. He had been gone for three days now, and he wouldn't be coming back.

She wished now that she'd ranted and raved and told him what she thought of his faithless behaviour, but at the time, the news that he was leaving her for someone else had been so unexpected that the shock had rendered her almost speechless.

For the twentieth time she reviewed in her mind the events of the past week. Sandie had given in at last and let the cat out of the bag. Mickey had listened calmly, frozen-faced.

'What are you going to do now?' Sandie asked, when the whole sorry mess was exposed at last.

'Do? What do you think? Have it out with him, of course! I don't have to put up with any of this.'

'Then just make sure this is what you really want. If the pair of you break up now there may be no going back.'

'It's either this or lie down and be a doormat for Tom and this woman to walk all over. When he comes through that door after work tonight I'll be waiting for him!'

True to her word, Mickey tackled him before she could have second thoughts. At first Tom didn't understand that he was in big trouble.

'What's to eat? I don't smell anything cooking. Or were we meant to be going out, and I've forgotten?'

'Something is cooking, all right, Tom Bowman, and it's your goose!'

'What? I don't get it. Don't play games, Mickey. I'm too tired. You wouldn't believe the day I've had.'

'Your girlfriend giving you a hard time, is she?'

A wary look came into his eyes. 'I don't know what you mean.'

'Then perhaps you could explain this!' She thrust the receipt at him, and after glancing at it he began to bluster.

'How dare you spy on me, Mickey? I'd have thought better of you than this. Surely you knew I have to be pleasant to people I'm meant to be instructing? That's what the job is all about — public relations.'

'To the point where you have to take the clients to Bournemouth for the weekend?'

'It didn't mean anything,' he said sulkily.

'Perhaps not to you, but it means everything to me, Tom Bowman! I can't bear the thought that you lied to me over this, and how do I know how many lies have been told in the past?'

From there on it was all downhill. 'If you don't trust me there's no point in us staying together,' he snapped. 'I'll get my things together now and get out of your hair. I won't stay around where I'm not wanted.'

'Good!' She was determined not to give him the satisfaction of hearing her beg, and she certainly wasn't prepared to back down.

'I'll take my share of the Australia money out of our joint account,' he went on. 'We'll split it down the middle, fifty, fifty, right?'

'Fine!' That was the final twist of the knife. Expecting that he might say that, she'd gone to the bank and taken out all the money she herself had contributed, scrupulously correct down to the last penny. All that remained was the few pounds Tom had put in, and he was lucky to get that!

She managed to hold herself together at work, treating the clients with her customary courtesy, and it wasn't until her mother checked in with her weekly phone call that she fell apart.

'Is anything wrong, dear? You sound a bit distant.'

'Oh, Mum!' It all came tumbling out then, the evenings when Tom was supposed to be working late, the lies he'd told, and finally, his weekend in Bournemouth, presumably with the lovely Felicity.

'I'm so sorry,' Joyce Clarke murmured. 'As you know, we liked Tom and were pleased to welcome him into the family. I don't know how we could have been so wrong about him.'

'You and me both! Oh, Mum, it hurts so much! I just don't know what I'm going to do!'

'Well, I'll tell you this for nothing, my girl. If he comes crawling back, don't you believe a word of it. What he's done once he can do again. Believe me, you're well out of it.'

'Then why do I still love him so much?'

'I know, darling, I know! But things will get better, I promise! Look, what you need is a change of scene. Why don't you come out here to us as planned? I expect we can rustle up a few pounds to help with buying your ticket.'

'Thanks, Mum, that's very kind, but I don't think that would be a good idea at the moment, do you?'

Joyce sighed. She could guess what her daughter was thinking. The Australian holiday was supposed to have been what amounted to a honeymoon trip. How could poor Mickey bear to travel out there on her own? It would only emphasise her loss.

They rang off, promising to keep in close touch. Joyce went in search of her husband, fuming. When he heard what had happened he shrugged his shoulders philosophically.

'Better to have found out now rather than later, love.'

'That's what I said, not that it helped. Naturally she'd rather not have found out at all. Or what I mean is, not have it happen at all.'

'Hmm, but at least this way she avoids a messy divorce.'

'Joe Clarke! I must say you're taking

this very calmly! The poor girl is absolutely shattered!'

Her husband smiled wryly. 'Well of course I'd like to knock him down and jump all over him, but he isn't here, is he? So there's no point in my getting all worked up. It'll only bring on a heart attack.'

He turned back to his newspaper, but Joyce could tell he was trying not to show he was upset. She grinned at the idea of her even-tempered husband resorting to violence, but it was too bad they weren't back in the good old days, when a father could thrash a cad and get away with it.

She brushed away a tear. If there was anything worse than having a romance go pear-shaped, it was being a parent, having to watch a beloved daughter go through that misery. This was happening to Mickey now, and there was absolutely nothing her mother could do about it.

Sandie wasn't about to let her best friend sit at home, moping. 'Come on, there's a new club in town. Want to give it a try?'

'No, I don't!'

'Why not? It'd do you good to dance the night away.'

Mickey groaned. 'Or hold up the bar, I suppose, chatting up dreadful men who are cheating on their wives and girlfriends!'

'How about a film, then?' Sandie didn't give up easily. Mickey pulled a face.

'All I want to do is go home, change into my sweats and put my feet up.'

'Fine. Then we'll rent a video and get a take-away.'

Deep inside, Mickey knew that Sandie had the right idea. When she was on her own she found herself waiting for the phone to ring, even picking it up to see if it was working properly. She knew that her mother was right; Tom couldn't be trusted so even if he did come round, full of contrition, she shouldn't let him back into her life. But how could she possibly turn him away, when she still loved him so much?

Sandie was a good friend, but she would keep muttering old clichés, such as getting right back on the horse after you fell off. If this meant immediately starting up another relationship, she could forget it. Mickey certainly wasn't ready for that.

She glanced at herself in the mirror. Her skin looked muddy and her hair was lank. Maybe she should take Sandie's advice and go for a new hairdo and a facial. It wouldn't do to let herself go.

'We're going ice skating tonight, and you're coming with us,' Sandie announced at work the next day.

'Oh, no you don't! I've tried that before and never managed to stay upright for more than two seconds at a time. I don't have the right sort of balance or something.'

'Nonsense! Brendan and I will hold you up, and if you do fall down, better a few bruises on the derriere than a bruised heart.'

'Oh, all right, then, but if I spoil the

evening for the two of you, don't say I didn't warn you.'

As it happened, the evening could have been worse. Mickey fell once, but was soon hauled back on her feet by the other two. Then she shuffled along gingerly, holding on to the boards, while Sandie and Brendan sailed off in time to the music. It was good to wallow in some mindless pleasure.

There were a few tense moments later, though, when they were sitting in the snack bar devouring burgers and enormous milkshakes. Brendan was a nice enough young man, but tactless with it.

'I saw that man of yours with his new girlfriend,' he remarked, gazing up at the price list to see if he wanted more to eat.

'Brendan!' Sandie hissed, but he frowned at her in puzzlement.

'What? I only said . . . '

'What were they doing?' Mickey asked, driven by some awful compulsion to torture herself by knowing the worst.

'Doing? Nothing much. Just looking in shop windows in the High Street.'

'What sort of shop windows?' Mickey couldn't forget the times she and Tom had done the same. Looking at furniture they couldn't afford, planning their future home. Admiring diamond rings in display in the jeweller's.

Tom favoured a big solitaire, but Mickey fancied three small stones in a crown setting.

Brendan yelped suddenly. 'What did you do that for?' He glared at Sandie, who glared back.

'It's all right, Sandie. I'm bound to run into them myself sometime. In a town this size it'd be hard to avoid them.' Mickey turned to Brendan. 'What did you think of her, then, this Felicity? Nice looking, is she?'

'Phwoar!' he responded, wide-eyed.

Mickey couldn't help smiling at what she thought of as a typical male response. It sounded as though Felicity had everything going for her. Attractive to men as well as coming from a wealthy family. How could Mickey compete with that?

'I wonder where he's staying now?' she murmured, unable to stop herself.

'It's best you don't know!' Sandie said firmly. 'Then you can't show up there, pleading with him to come back to you.'

'Alexandra Lomax! Shame on you! I'd do no such thing. I've got more pride than that. Anyhow, if I did want to speak to him I could find him at the Club. Presumably he still works there.'

'Oh, yes, he does, but he's moved in beside Felicity now.

'She's got one of those fancy new flats in that converted mill down by the river.'

'Thank you, Brendan! Thank you very much!'

'What have I said now?' He looked pained at the sarcasm in Sandie's tone and Mickey felt it was time to intervene, or her romance wouldn't be the only one on the rocks.

'It's been lovely, you guys, but I must

be going. I think a nice long soak in the bath is called for, before I stiffen up too much.' She stood up, and Sandie got to her feet as well, thrusting her arm into the sleeve of her jacket as she did so.

'Same here. We've got work tomorrow.'

★   ★   ★

Life went on much as usual as summer turned into autumn. Mickey's conversations with her mother were largely centred around the weather, for Joyce was intrigued by the seasons 'down under' which of course were the reverse of those in Britain.

'We're spending a lot of money just to talk about how much rain we've had,' Mickey laughed, but as both of them knew the important thing was to keep in touch, even while Joyce felt she was walking on egg shells.

'Have you found someone to share the flat with yet, dear?'

'I've been putting it off, Mum.' She

had thought of asking Sandie to move in, but her friend's relationship with Brendan seemed to be moving into a new stage and there seemed no point in changing the status quo only to have Sandie move out again in a short time.

'Your father and I have been talking, and we'd love to have you come to us at Christmas. No need to worry about the fare, that'll be our Christmas present to you.'

'I'm not sure, Mum.'

'Oh, but just imagine leaving a nasty British winter behind and spending the holiday season in an Australian summer.'

Mickey promised to think about it, but really she craved the comfort of a traditional white Christmas, shopping for presents on dark evenings, with the shops all brightly lit and inviting. She had suffered too many changes already and needed the security of what was tried and true.

Then something happened to jolt her out of her rut. One bright October morning Sandie looked up from her desk to find a tall, handsome man looking down on her. There was something about him which shrieked wealth and privilege. On the spur of the moment she couldn't decide whether it was his air of confidence, or his dark suit and highly polished shoes, items of apparel which certain hadn't come from shops in the High Street.

'Can I help you?' she asked, putting on her brightest smile.

'Would you happen to be Miss Michaela Clarke? I'm told she works here.'

'She's not in at the moment. Can I help?'

Mickey had gone to the bakery to fetch their mid-morning snacks and should be back at any moment, but Sandie was curious to know what this was all about so she kept the information to herself.

'I see. Well, I need to speak to her on a matter of some urgency, so I'd like her to call me as soon as she comes in, if she will.'

'Is it about an insurance settlement?' Sandie probed, but he merely pulled out his wallet and extracted a business card, which he handed to her.

'She'll find my number there. Please see that she receives this immediately.'

Sandie bridled at his manner, but she said, 'Of course,' and stood staring after him as he strode out of the office, not pausing to look back. What on earth was all that about? She glanced down at the embossed card. *Jerome Marshall*, it read, *partner in the firm of Marshall, Begby & Swann, Solicitors at Law*.

So he was a solicitor, but what did he want with Mickey? Sandie hoped fervently that her friend wasn't in for more trouble.

4

Mickey leaned back against her office chair, phone in hand, while Sandie watched with keen interest. She had expected to be placed on hold for far too long, forced to listen to muzak, but to her surprise the secretary at the other end told her that Mr Marshall had left instructions that she was to be put through to him at once, even if he was in conference.

'Miss Clarke. Good of you to get back to me so promptly.' His voice was pleasant. From his tone, he appeared to have been the product of a top-ranking school or university. 'I would like to arrange a meeting with you, and the sooner the better,' he went on.

'Can you tell me what this is about, please? I mean, I don't know you, and I haven't asked to see a solicitor.'

'I'd rather not say until I can speak to

you in person. Now, then, if you will give me your home address and suggest a time convenient to you, we can get matters rolling.'

Mickey frowned. A solicitor who made house calls? It sounded fishy to her.

'I'll be glad to come to your office,' she said primly, 'or we could meet here, or in a restaurant.'

'I'm sorry, Miss Clarke, but this is really quite hush hush. I can assure you that I'm quite trustworthy.'

Reluctantly, she gave him her address and they agreed to get together that evening.

'Are you mad?' Sandie shrieked, when Mickey filled her in. 'Letting a man you've never met into your flat?'

'You've met the man, Sandie. Did he seem like an axe murderer to you?'

'Well, no, but who knows what a murderer looks like when he's behaving normally? And what's this deep, dark secret all about? It sounds like something out of a spy novel!'

Mickey shrugged. 'Perhaps it's a case of mistaken identity. Someone else, with a name similar to mine, is getting sued for something.'

'Phooey. We work in an insurance office. You of all people should know it doesn't work like that. You might be served with a summons to appear in court, perhaps, but no solicitor is going to make an appointment to go to your home! What you should do, my girl, is to phone him right back and cancel. Tell him to write you a letter if he's so keen to go on with this!'

But strange though it was, Mickey resolved to go through with it. She was intrigued by the whole scenario and if she refused to see the man she knew she'd be on tenterhooks for days, worrying about what might be behind it all.

Sandie sniffed loudly when she heard this. 'All right, then. On your head be it. But you're not going to meet him all on your own. You'd be a sitting duck in that flat. I'm going to be there with you, and Brendan, too.'

'There's no need for Brendan to be there,' Mickey told her. 'Two of us will be quite enough. If he tries anything, you divert his attention awhile I turn the fire extinguisher on him. That'll cool him off!'

They chuckled, but even so Mickey found it hard to concentrate on her work for the rest of the day and Miss Phipps was forced to call her attention to her duties on more than one occasion.

* * *

'What do you think I should wear?' Mickey demanded, when they arrived at her flat.

'What you have on will do very nicely. No need to get all dressed up for this Marshall person.'

'But it would give me something to do while we're waiting.'

'Too late now!' Sandie said, as the

44

intercom buzzed. 'That'll be him now. Tell him to come up right away. The sooner we get this over with the better. Then we can bring in a nice Chinese takeaway and relax.'

Jerome Marshall was just as Sandie had described him — handsome, suave, exquisitely dressed. He stopped short on seeing that Mickey wasn't alone.

'I did say I wanted to keep this private,' he said crossly.

'I hope you didn't expect me to invite a stranger into my home when I'm all by myself,' she told him. 'That certainly wouldn't be wise in this day and age. Besides, Sandie is my friend. We can trust her to keep any confidential matters to herself.'

'Point taken,' he nodded. 'You can come up now!' he called over his shoulder, and Mickey's eyes opened wide when a tall, shapely redhead sidled into the room, leaving the door wide open, and proceeded to look around with barely concealed distaste.

'Why, you're that Felicity Smythe from

the golf club!' Sandie cried. 'Mickey, she's the one who stole Tom from you!'

'Then I'm surprised you'd show your face here,' Mickey said icily, as she closed the door, none too gently.

'My name's not Smythe. I'm Felicity Marshall, as you might know if you'd bothered to ask.' The girl swept her long auburn tresses over her shoulder in a sudden movement which would have cricked the neck of anyone less supple. It was the act of someone who loved to be the focus of attention.

Oh, no! Mickey could see it all now. She must be this Jerome's wife! Not content with stealing another girl's fiancée she had also walked out on her own relationship, and now her husband was after Tom Bowman. As a solicitor he would know how to deal with him in a non-violent way.

'If you're looking for Tom, you're out of luck. He isn't here. I haven't set eyes on him since he left me to go to this — this wife of yours!'

'My wife! I'm not married, Miss

46

Clarke. What made you think I was?'

Felicity laughed, tossing her head again. 'What a hoot! She thinks we're married, Jerry! He's my brother, not my husband!'

'But your name is Smythe,' Sandie interjected.

'No, it's not. Oh, I know, it's because I was staying with my aunt and uncle when I first moved to town. Aunt Rosalind is Mummy's sister. Quentin Smythe is my uncle by marriage, you see. Our uncle, that is, Jerry's and mine.'

'I'm glad we've got that settled,' Jerome snapped. 'Look, I wonder if we might all sit down? This is getting us nowhere.'

Mickey joined Sandie on the settee and their visitors chose chairs nearby.

'It's imperative that we find Tom Bowman as quickly as possible, and since no-one seems to know where he is, we thought we'd better start here.'

Mickey shook her head. 'I've told you, I haven't seen him for ages. Try the golf club, that's where he works.'

Now it was Felicity's turn to shake her head. 'He left his job there. I haven't seen him for days, although his things are still in my flat.'

'Now you know how I felt when he left me to go to you!' Mickey told her. 'I can't pretend I feel sorry for you after you persuaded my fiance to go off with you.'

'But he told me the two of you hadn't been getting along for some time, and that your relationship was already over when you threw him out of the flat!'

Mickey fumed at the thought of how Tom had twisted the sequence of events to fit his purpose. 'I made him leave after I found out about the two of you carrying on, spending the weekend in Bournemouth together without my knowledge, when he was supposed to be marrying me! He'd lied to me time and again, and I wasn't having any more of it!'

Jerome put up a warning hand.

'Ladies, ladies, please! I can see that you both have an axe to grind here. Both of you have obviously been taken in and treated badly by Bowman. What we have to do now is try some damage control.'

'Control!' Mickey snorted. 'The damage is already done, at least as far as I'm concerned. I don't know what he's done to Felicity here, but it can hardly be any worse.'

'I'm afraid it can. Possibly you're aware that we come from a wealthy family. On reaching the age of twenty-one, my sister came into a substantial amount of money from a trust fund. It appears that your Mr Bowman has managed to relieve her of a very large part of that inheritance, and that is why we have to act at once, before it's too late to retrieve that money.'

Mickey was aghast. 'Tom may be many things, but I'm sure he's not a thief,' she told him. 'And how would he get hold of your money in the first place?' she demanded of Felicity.

'Interest rates are so low, and he told me he knew how to invest my money so I'd get a much higher return, up to twenty-five percent a year. That's why I gave it to him.'

5

Sandie's eyes opened wide. She'd be the first to admit that she was no financial expert, but she did read magazines, and she knew that Felicity must be particularly naïve if she expected a twenty-five per cent return on her money. Either that, or she was extremely greedy!

'How much money has Tom er, borrowed?' she asked. Not that it was her business, but Mickey would want to know and would be too polite to enquire.

'A quarter of a million,' Felicity muttered, carefully avoiding her brother's eye.

Sandie was stunned into silence. No wonder Jerome was looking so grim!

'But where has it actually gone?' Mickey wanted to know. 'I mean, it's a lot of money to put in one place, and

I'm sure Tom knows nothing about the stock market. Perhaps he invested in some business or other, such as a golf club that wants to start up.'

'Or perhaps he backed a horse with a wooden leg!' Jerome snapped. 'One way or another, he took advantage of my idiot sister and now all her money has disappeared into the blue!'

Felicity cast a furious look at her brother. 'I am not an idiot, Jerry, and don't you dare say I am!'

'That's a matter of opinion, old girl!'

The situation was getting out of hand and Mickey hastened to stop them sniping at each other.

'What on earth will you do if you can't get the money back?' she asked. She had never expected to find herself in sympathy with Felicity, but now they were seemingly the innocent victims of the same man it put a different complexion on things.

Felicity shrugged. 'Daddy will help me, I expect. He's sitting on a bundle, he'll make sure I get my share.'

Sandie was disgusted. She knew she should keep quiet, but she couldn't help herself. 'If you already had a quarter of a million, why on earth did you want more?'

The other girl stared at her, a look of exasperation on her pretty face. 'A quarter of a million goes nowhere nowadays. It won't even buy you a decent house! There was no way I could live the rest of my life on that amount, so when Tom said he knew how to improve on it I trusted him. That's all.'

You could have got a job like the rest of us have to do, Sandie thought, but probably the spoilt girl wouldn't know what work was. She would flit through life like a pampered butterfly until her adoring father died, when she would inherit even more money from him. Now the poor man was left to pick up the pieces.

'I'm really distressed by all this,' Mickey remarked, turning to face Jerome, 'but there's really nothing I can do to help, and frankly, I don't know why you bothered to come. I could have told you over the phone that I have no idea where Tom is now. You've have a wasted journey.'

'So you say,' Felicity sneered. 'Personally, I think you were in it together!'

'What!'

'Isn't it obvious? Both of you had dead-end jobs, but you wanted more out of life. Then I came along, and Tom saw his chance.

'Oh, I can see it all now, the two of you sitting here in this room, plotting and planning. He'd pretend to leave you and make me fall for him, then when he'd taken all my money the two of you would ride off into the sunset, laughing all the way!'

'Here, steady on, old girl!' Alarmed, Jerome put a hand on his sister's arm, but she shook him off.

'Don't tell me she's taken you in as well, Jerry! Why, I just bet she's the brains behind it all. That stupid Tom Bowman couldn't have thought up this scam all by himself!'

Listening to this outburst, Mickey felt a cold fury rising up inside her. She felt like taking the girl by the throat and throttling her, but that wouldn't help the situation. She forced herself to speak calmly.

'Feel free to search the flat, if that's what you think! Be sure to take up the floorboards in case the money is hidden underneath, and don't miss the airing cupboard because Tom could be hiding in there!'

'I wasn't born yesterday! By now you'll have the money in a Swiss bank account or somewhere. As for Tom, he's lying low until all the fuss dies down, and then he'll sneak back here like the lying dog he is. Well, you just listen to me; you won't get away with this, Minnie Clarke, or whatever your name is! Jerry won't let you.'

Mickey stood up, her head held high. 'I'd like you both to leave, please. I've told you the truth, and no amount of bullying is going to make me say anything different.'

Felicity started to say something, but her brother put his hand on her shoulder and gave her a warning look as he propelled her towards the door.

'Thank you for your time, Miss Clarke. You'll be hearing from me again.'

The door closed behind them and the sound of their footsteps died away.

'Ouch! That was dreadful!' Mickey shuddered.

'It certainly was! Look at you, you're shaking like a leaf. I'm going to make you a cup of tea, all right?'

Nodding, Mickey curled up on the settee, hugging a cushion to her chest. When the tea came she sipped it gratefully, thankful that Sandie had been here to offer support.

'That awful, awful girl!' Sandie muttered. 'If you ask me, she deserved all she got!'

'But a quarter of a million pounds, Sandie. I can't even imagine owning so much money at one time, can you? I wonder if it's true; about Tom, I mean.

Has he just snatched the money and run off with it? He has his faults, but I can't see him as the type who'd rob a poor little pensioner of her life savings, or anything like that.'

'No, he may have a conscience, up to a point, but Felicity is hardly a poor old woman, is she? And the impression I got is that her pride is hurt more than her pocket. Whatever happens, Daddy will always be there to bail her out. It could be that Tom realised that and gave into temptation, knowing that she wouldn't be out on the street without a penny.

'Anyway, he couldn't have spent it all at once. There's a pretty good chance they'll get at least some of it back. This Jerome is a solicitor, so he'll know the right way to go about it. I'm sure he's already been in touch with the police.'

'Oh, no! I suppose they'll be on my doorstep next! I hate all this, Sandie! I bet they'll want to look at my bank accounts to see if I've been socking away large sums of money. If this gets out I could lose my job, and then where will I be?'

'I'm sure it won't come to that,' Sandie soothed. 'They can't pin anything on you if you're innocent: because you're innocent, I mean,' she added hastily.

'Mud sticks.'

'Never mind thinking that way. I tell you what, though. What if Tom didn't really mean to defraud Felicity? Maybe he was just stupid.'

'What do you mean?'

'Well, say he put all the money into some risky investment — futures, say — and it failed. That's been known to happen, and it has nothing to do with fraud, although of course whoever is behind the scheme might still be crooks. Tom could have placed the money somewhere in good faith and then had a terrible shock when it all went pear-shaped.'

'So then why has he disappeared?'

'Because he can't face Felicity, of course.'

'I suppose it's possible.' Mickey cradled the warm cup in her hands as she mulled over what her friend had said. She had loved Tom — still had feelings for him — and she hated to think that she had been so mistaken in him. He'd been unfaithful and a liar, but surely not a wicked conman who would surely end up with a stiff prison sentence when the law caught up with him. She said as much to Sandie.

'It's just like you to make excuses for the man,' Sandie snorted. 'Even if he's not a crook, he's certainly been pretty stupid. Even I know that the higher the anticipated return, the more risky the venture. People who play the stock market are warned never to invest more than they can afford to lose.'

6

There's been an important development. I'd like to call round and see you. I could come right away if that would be convenient for you.'

Mickey's heart sank as she realised that it was Jerome Marshall on the phone. It was several days after the confrontation at her flat, and she had been feeling jittery ever since.

'I'm sorry, but it isn't. I can't have visitors at work, Mr Marshall.' In fact, employees weren't even supposed to take personal calls, unless it was a case of emergency, and Miss Phipps was already fixing Mickey with a gimlet eye.

'I understand. Have lunch with me today, then.' As she hesitated, he went on, 'It really is terribly important, or I wouldn't dream of pressing you. Name the time and place, and I'll be there waiting.'

'All right, you win. Let's say the Copper Kettle at noon?' Ignoring Sandie's raised eyebrows, she replaced the phone in its cradle and bent over her work.

True to his word, the solicitor was there before her, looking smart in his customary working gear of suit and tie. Mickey was glad that she'd chosen to wear her best grey skirt and silk blouse that morning. Having felt the need to cheer herself up with a bit of colour she'd added the pretty scarf that Tom had brought back from Bournemouth.

When he'd gone away she'd thrown it in the bin as a gesture of defiance, but had taken it out again in a fit of guilt, thinking she might as well get some use from it, and if wearing it made her feel badly she could always donate it to a charity shop.

'I went ahead and nabbed us a table,' Jerome announced. 'I've been here before and I know how quickly the place fills up.'

He led the way to a table for two by

the window, and a waitress in a green overall immediately leapt to his side, holding out two leather covered menus. Either he was a favourite customer or the woman recognised him as someone to be reckoned with.

Mickey had expected him to start in at once on whatever the big news was, but he kept the conversation light and general, much as a man might do on a first date with somebody he didn't know very well. Perhaps he was sizing her up, although the questions he asked weren't likely to tell him much about the case in hand. Had she grown up in the town; what were her parents doing in Australia; did she enjoy her work in the insurance business.

In turn she asked him what sort of legal work he took on; what his interests were; did he enjoy sports.

Finally, with a feeling of regret, she looked at her watch. 'I'm so sorry, but I'm due back at work, and you haven't told me why we're here, why it was so important for us to meet today.'

'Ah, yes. Well, as I expect you must understand, I've reported Felicity's problem to the police. At first they seemed disinclined to get involved, saying it was a domestic matter and that partners frequently disagree over money. As a solicitor I should advise my sister to make a claim against Tom Bowman in a civil court. However, when I explained that it was a case of fraud, involving a great deal of money, they changed their tune. Money talks, I'm afraid.'

He sounded apologetic, and Mickey realised that he wasn't so much referring to the amount of Felicity's loss, but to the fact that he came from a wealthy background which had probably impressed the constable who was taking note of the problem. Then, too, Jerome was a solicitor, which meant he had a certain standing when it came to the law.

'The first thing they did was to see if Tom has 'form' as the officer put it. Of course, that's not difficult these days when everything is computerised, giving the police access to all sorts of records in other jurisdictions. That's the good news. The bad news, at least as far as Felicity is concerned, is that Tom has no criminal record.'

'I could have told you that!' Mickey sounded indignant and Jerome's lips quirked in a smile, which came and went like the sun between showers on a blustery day.

'Your loyalty does you credit, although the man doesn't deserve it,' he replied. 'You may think you know Tom Bowman, but you must admit that we're entitled to a different viewpoint, given what's happened here.'

'I suppose so, but why couldn't you have told me this over the phone?'

'Because as I said, there's been a development. When I got nowhere with the police I went online and surfed the net, seeing if I could find any clues that way. You wouldn't believe how many Tom Bowmans there are in the world! I was just about to give up when I came across a web site put up by a woman called Lydia Frew, who says she's been defrauded by her ex-fiancé, Tom Bowman, who had run off with her savings.

'There is a very clear photo of the man on that site, and as Felicity is out of town, I've brought you a printout to see if you can identify our hero. As you may know, I've never met him myself.'

Feeling slightly sick, Mickey accepted the page he held out and was dismayed to see Tom's smiling face looking up at her.

'Well, is it the right Tom Bowman?'

She nodded. 'Is this legal? Isn't it libel or something if you post accusations on the web?'

He shrugged. 'Unfortunately a great many things find their way online which shouldn't be there, but in cases like this the perpetrator can get away with it unless the so-called victim takes legal action. And of course if Bowman is guilty he isn't likely to come forward; that's if he knows about it at all.'

This was all too much. Mickey closed her eyes wearily. Seeing her distress, Jerome stood up and held out his hand to help her. 'Come on, I'll see you back to your office. And I want you to take this piece with you and read it carefully. Something may occur to you then, which will give us some clues.'

She had no chance to read it until mid-afternoon, when Miss Phipps announced that she had to go to the dentist, but would be back as soon as possible. When the coast was clear, Mickey whipped out the paper Jerome had given her and skimmed through it, ignoring Sandie's wild signals from across the room.

Lydia Frew looked to be a few years older than Tom, at least to go by the small photo of her which the woman had included. Tom's picture was much larger so that anyone opening the web site would notice it at once. There was no telling where the woman lived as only an e-mail address was provided; presumably she didn't want the world beating a path to her door.

Her pathetic story was there for all to see, written in the style of one of those true confessions magazines. She was an only child who had never married, having stayed at home to look after elderly parents.

Although not wealthy, the older couple owned a pleasant house in an area where properties were highly sought after. They promised Lydia that one day the house would be hers, along with their substantial savings, if she devoted her life to them instead of placing them in a nursing home when the time came.

All went according to plan. They were a loving family, and when the old people become too unwell to be left alone, Lydia gladly gave up her office job and stayed home with them until they eventually died. Then she took stock of her life.

At thirty-five she was still young enough to find happiness with a husband and children. If that didn't happen, then the money from the sale of the family home, carefully invested, would provide her with a comfortable income in her retirement years. Meanwhile, she would pick up where she left off and return to work.

'What on earth are you reading, Mickey? You look as sick as a donkey!'

Mickey came to with a start. 'Oh, Sandie. Jerome Marshall found this on the internet. Some woman has posted a picture of Tom there, along with some rigmarole about him doing her out of her savings. Unbelievable!'

'Sounds sort of familiar, eh?'

'And look here, she says they met at a golf club, where he was the pro, giving her lessons, and they fell in love.'

'Where? What golf club?'

'She doesn't say. Oh, Sandie, all this seems like a bad dream to me.'

7

You'd better come home with me,'
Sandie said, as they were getting ready
to leave the office. 'We've got a lot to
talk about. I'll make my famous
vegetarian lasagne and we'll open a
bottle of wine. How about it?'

Mickey agreed. Her mind was in a
whirl and she felt that if she didn't
empty out all the confusing thoughts,
her head would burst! Later, when they
were starting on their second glass of
wine, and the flat was filled with the
delicious aroma of cheese, tomato,
courgettes and mushrooms, Sandie
returned to the subject.

'Have you ever heard of this Lydia
woman before, Mickey? Did Tom ever
mention her?'

'I've been trying to remember, but I
don't think so. Actually, when we were
together we didn't discuss old flames.

69

We just assumed that both of us would have had previous relationships of some sort. After all, I'd been out with several chaps before I met Tom.

'The fact remains that she knows Tom! She must do, or how else would she have got hold of his photo?'

'Still . . . What if their affair, or whatever it was, was all one-sided? Or they were just casual acquaintances? She might have read more into it than there really was, and when Tom set her straight she wanted to get her revenge. A woman scorned, and all that. So she makes up this story to embarrass him.'

'You're forgetting one thing. Felicity! Is it likely that two unrelated women would come up with the same yarn if it wasn't true? Surely you're not suspecting some conspiracy between them?'

Mickey stood up and began to pace around the room which, given its small size, wasn't easy. 'I don't know what to think! I'm only glad that I didn't have any money for him to misuse, that's all.' A small, nagging voice inside her head reminded her of their Australian fund. He would have cleaned that out if she hadn't had the presence of mind to remove her own share before their showdown.

The oven timer pinged. 'Come on, let's eat!' Sandie announced, and they spent the next half hour eating their food while they chatted about everyday things. It was only when they were lingering over coffee that she brought up the subject again.

'I suppose you can start to move on now. Forget about Tom, and let those other women fight over him.'

Mickey opened her eyes wide. 'Oh, no, I shan't do that! I want to get to the bottom of this, for my own peace of mind. Don't you see, Tom has told me so many lies that I want to know what else has been hidden from me before I can put all this behind me.'

'You'll only get hurt in the process,' Sandie warned.

'I've been hurt already. If I can find out what a rotter he really is, it'll help me get over him, don't you think?'

'Well, if that's what you really want. I suppose the first thing we need to do is talk to this Lydia Frew. Where does she live, anyway?'

'She doesn't say. There's only an e-mail address on her website.'

'Then that's where you start. Write and say you've been victimised by Tom Bowman as well, and can you get together.'

'I'll think about it, but I bet she'll have heard from dozens of people by now. Not that I think he's ripped off that many women, but she's bound to hear from some cranks.'

'She could be right here in town, you know.' Sandie mused. 'If she met him when he was giving her golf lessons that could be at our local club.'

'I'm not sure,' Mickey murmured. 'He hadn't been in town too long when we first met, or so he said. He told me he'd come from Huddersfield and of course I took that at face value, but for all I know that might have been another lie. Surely someone would have known, and said something, if he'd lived locally for any length of time.'

'There's one way to find out if she was ever here,' Sandie said. 'As you know, Brendan is a member of the club. I'll get him to look up the appointment book to see if anyone called Lydia Frew has taken lessons in the past year. Meanwhile, you contact her by e-mail and ask if you can meet.'

'Yes, but not tonight. It's getting late, and I really should be going.'

She stood up, rather unsteadily. The food and coffee had done little to soak up all the wine she'd had and the room was beginning to blur.

'You'd better stay the night,' Sandie told her. 'You can go to work from here.'

Mickey accepted gratefully. Rain was lashing against the windows and the thought of going out into the wet and standing at the bus stop wasn't inviting.

★　★　★

'That young man of yours was here again, looking for you,' Miss Phipps said frostily, when the girls arrived at the office, full of apologies. Their bus had been full up and had sailed past without stopping, and they had been forced to wait another twenty minutes, which made them late. 'I do wish you girls would keep your private lives well away from the office. You are here to work, not make assignations.'

'Tom was here?' Mickey squeaked. Now what was she going to do? Turn him over to the police?

'How do I know what his name is? I can't keep up with you girls and your friends. By his voice, I should say it's that chap who telephoned you the other day. And that's another thing. You know the rules, I really can't . . . '

Mickey tuned out. So it was Jerome, then. What did he want now? She waited until Miss Phipps had disappeared into the loo to repair her make-up and then she tried to phone him, but a secretary told her he was out on business, so that was that.

'I'll pop over to his office in the lunch hour and leave him a note,' she told Sandie, out of the side of her mouth as Miss Phipps returned to her desk. 'There may be new developments.'

'Send him a fax,' Sandie hissed in return, but Mickey knew that Phippsie would disapprove, and she didn't know his e-mail address, so that was that.

Luckily he was in his office when she arrived, shortly after noon. She was surprised to find him eating sandwiches at his desk. He didn't strike her as the type who would bring a packed lunch from home, but he probably patronised a nearby establishment which provided take away lunches for office workers.

'I called at your flat last night,' he told her, 'but you were out.'

'Oh, I stayed with my friend, Sandie, and went to work from there,' she answered, not that it was any of his business where she spent her evenings. 'We had rather a late night and I didn't fancy getting soaked on the way home.'

'Would you like a sandwich? These are really quite good.'

'Oh, no, thank you. What did you want to see me about? Have the police found Tom?'

'No, no, nothing like that. I just happened to be passing by and called in on the off chance, to see if you'd like to have dinner with me.'

'That was kind,' Mickey managed to say. She was confused by the sudden change of direction. This was not what she had expected.

'I enjoyed our lunch together the other day, Michaela, and I'd like to get to know you better. So how about it, shall we make a date?'

As she walked back to the office, she could just imagine the look on Sandie's face when she found out that Mickey had a date with the handsome solicitor! Not that she herself had any illusions about his interest in her. After being let down by Tom she had become cynical about men.

Jerome probably wanted to get close

to her to pick up on any clues she might drop accidentally, because he wanted to help his sister, not because he fancied Mickey for her own charms. Well, two could play at that game!

Jerome Marshall was looking forward to his dinner date with Mickey Clarke, or Michaela, as he preferred to think of her. That name conjured up visions of an elegant, confident woman, somewhat at variance with the young employee of an insurance company.

He was no snob, but he was used to mixing in fairly exclusive circles, where the women either had money, or high-powered careers, or both. Perhaps that was why he was intrigued by Mickey, who was quite different from the ladies he usually took out.

In the beginning he had inclined towards his sister's view, that Mickey had been working hand in glove with Tom to defraud Felicity of her money, but he soon summed her up as being transparently honest, someone who had herself been used by Tom and discarded when he moved on, scenting better prospects.

Then, too, she had behaved with dignity, keeping her cool even when Felicity flew off the handle, making all sorts of accusations. He also admired her for staying on in England after Tom had dumped her. It would have been much simpler for her to have flown off to Australia, to be with her sympathetic parents.

'So where's he taking you?' Sandie demanded, as the pair of them rummaged through Mickey's meagre wardrobe, trying to find something suitable for her to wear on her big date.

'*The Golden Door*, he says.'

Sandie whistled. 'That'll cost him a bob or two! That place is only for the idle rich.'

'Well, we know he's one of them, don't we? If Felicity inherited all that money, I don't suppose her brother would have been left out of the loop. Added to that, he's a solicitor, so he must make good money.'

'Mmm. You'll have to tell me all about it tomorrow. Otherwise the only way I'll ever get to know what it's like inside is if I stand outside the window with my nose pressed to the glass.'

'You and Brendan should go. If you just have a starter and then leave you should be able to afford it!'

'They probably have a cover charge,' Sandie said gloomily. 'No, I think I'd rather rely on you. I don't feel like splurging a week's wages on half an avocado.'

In spite of her determination not to feel overawed by the experience, Mickey found herself impressed by the ambience of *The Golden Door*. It was the kind of place where you had to wait to be seated, but as soon as they put their noses inside the door a maitre d' sprang forward, greeting Jerome by name. He was obviously well known here.

'Your table is ready, Mr Marshall, sir.' He led the way up red-carpeted stairs to an upper level which over-looked the main restaurant. The walls were covered with dark panelling, on which rather good paintings were displayed at intervals.

As had Mickey expected, the tables were spread with real table cloths, woven from some sort of misty blue fabric. The matching napkins were generously-sized, and folded to look like swans' heads.

Mickey glanced around at the other diners, all of whom seemed to be well to do, to judge by their garments and expensive hair styles. What would it be like to come to such a place on a regular basis, she wondered? Would she always feel such delight, or would it pall in time?

'Ah, thank you.' Jerome accepted the over-sized menu the waiter handed him before the man handed a similar dark blue folder to her, with a ceremonial bow. Mickey experienced a moment of panic when she realised that no prices were shown on the copy she had received. How was she supposed to know what she should order?

Luckily, Jerome sensed her hesitation. 'Is there anything you particularly fancy, or would you care to have me order for both of us?'

'That would be lovely,' she murmured. 'I do like most things, but no snails, please!'

He smiled. 'No escargots, then.' He signalled to the waiter, who had been hovering nearby, and proceeded to order several courses. 'And send me the sommelier, please.'

'Of course, sir. Right away.'

Mickey's eyes widened slightly. Asked to translate, she would have guessed it to be something that hung from the ceiling, like a sort of chandelier, perhaps, but she was glad she'd kept quiet when the wine waiter arrived. Jerome deftly ordered bottles of wine to accompany various courses and he went through the ritual of tasting and approving each one as she looked on in fascination.

As they went on with their leisurely meal, Mickey felt that she ought to show an interest in her host, and as his work was probably confidential she decided to ask about his family instead.

'I understand that your father has a number of factories,' she began. 'Is that a family tradition?'

Jerome regarded her closely for a long moment. She wasn't the first girl to have probed into that; in some cases a little gold digger had tried to work out how much he was worth. But no; as far as he could see Mickey had no hidden agenda.

'It started out with my great grandfather,' he explained. 'He had a small factory, making uniforms for the army, and when the Boer War broke out he suddenly found himself with more orders than he could handle. He borrowed money and opened a second establishment, and it all went on from there. It was a risk, of course, but he was an astute businessman and in time he was able to diversify, and from then on everything he touched turned to gold.'

'And that was where Felicity's inheritance came from?'

Again he hesitated, and Mickey was afraid she'd been impertinent, but he obviously decided that she could be trusted with the information, for in a moment he went on.

'By that time old Joshua Marshall had a family, and naturally he wanted to pass on to them the wealth he'd worked so hard to amass. However, he didn't want them to be so used to living in luxury that they'd squander their inheritance, and neither did he want the government to get their hands on it by way of taxation. So, he set up a family trust, in which each generation could receive income without withdrawing capital.'

'I see,' Mickey nodded, although she had only a vague idea of how these things worked.

'By the time our generation came on the scene, my grandfather had worked out a scheme whereby I and my male cousins would receive a tidy sum on our twenty-first birthdays, and the girls would get the same when they turned twenty-five.'

Mickey frowned. 'I don't understand. Why the difference?'

'The old boy was rather Victorian in outlook and he had the idea that girls should be protected from 'charming rogues' as he put it. He felt that girls matured later than their brothers and shouldn't be given money until they were sensible enough to keep a tight grip on it.'

'What a potty idea!' Mickey spluttered.

'This was Mother's feeling exactly. She felt that it was totally unfair to Felicity so she prevailed upon old Swann, who was head of our firm long before I joined it, to find a way to break the trust to an extent where my sister would inherit when she reached her twenty-first birthday. I'm told that he did so with the greatest reluctance, but as the Marshalls were among his most important clients he did what Mother wanted.

'Sadly, as things have turned out, the old boy was right all along. Felicity has found her 'charming rogue' and unless I'm very much mistaken, her money has all gone down the drain.'

'That's terrible! Your parents must be so distressed.'

'Oh, it could be worse, I suppose. We'll inherit more after our parents pass on, which, I sincerely hope and trust, will be many years from now. Meanwhile, let's not waste a lovely evening thinking gloomy thoughts.'

By the time they had each selected a delectable offering from the dessert trolley, and waited for coffee to arrive, Mickey was in a mellow mood, wishing that she could sit at this table forever, as the soft music played on.

Later, she sank back in the soft leather passenger seat of his car and closed her eyes. It had been an enchanted evening, and she felt that she'd better reach home soon before Jerome's Jaguar turned back into a pumpkin!

When he got out of the car to escort her to her door, she wondered what she should say if he asked to come in, but he made no move in that direction. Instead, he gently tilted up her chin and placed a long, lingering kiss on her unresisting lips. Then he bounded down the steps, eased himself into his car, and drove off.

8

How are you, dear? Feeling any better, are you?' Hearing her mother's anxious tones, Mickey realised with a start of surprise that it had been quite some time since she had brooded over Tom's defection. Anger over the awful things he'd done to the women he'd allegedly bilked and the knowledge that she herself was only one in a line of women he'd pretended to love, had swept away the pain she'd experienced on being abandoned. And then there was her new found feeling for Jerome, which flickered inside her like the flame of a small candle, bravely burning in the night.

'You're behind the times, Mum!'

'What do you mean, dear? Don't tell me that you and Tom are back together? Is that wise? What he can do once he'll do again and . . . '

'Mum, stop! No, we certainly won't be doing that! In fact, he's turned out to be someone quite different from what we all thought. That girl he went to after he left me, well, now she's been left in the lurch as well.'

'No!'

'Worse than that, he's somehow got his hands on all her money and either stolen it or lost it all on the stock market or something. I believe I mentioned that she's quite wealthy. Or was!'

Expressions of shock floated over the phone lines. 'And listen, Mum, have you got a pencil handy? There's a website I want you to look at, and tell me what you think.'

Obediently, Joyce made a note of the web address, then listened in horror as Mickey told her about Lydia Frew.

'Your father was quite right when he said you've had a narrow escape, dear. I don't know how all of us could have been so taken in by him. We liked him so much and were happy to welcome him into the family, and now we learn that he's nothing but a charming confidence trickster! Well, there's nothing more you can do about all this, dear, so you must move on now and try to forget all abut him.'

'That's what Sandie says.'

'Dear Sandie. How is she, anyway?'

'Oh, her usual jolly self. She's been a tower of strength through all this. I don't know what I'd have done without her.'

There was a pause, and then Joyce asked casually. 'I don't suppose you've met somebody new?'

'Well, I have been out with a chap a few times, as it happens.'

This provoked a flood of questions, but Mickey refused to be drawn. 'It's early days, Mum, and I don't want to rush into anything, OK?'

'That's probably wise, dear.' Joyce went on to tell about her own doings in Australia, and the conversation ended on a happy note, with the usual admonitions to keep in touch. They both had e-mail, of course, but they much preferred to hear each other's voices, for mother and daughter had always been close.

Mickey was still a little wary about her involvement with Jerome. In addition to the strong physical attraction she had begun to feel secure when in his company. Was she falling in love with him? She asked herself that question and wasn't sure of the answer. On top of that she didn't know if it was safe for her to place her trust in him. Or not yet, anyway. Only time would tell if that was the right thing to do.

Forthright Sandie told her to be careful. 'How do you know he's not using you, Mickey? Just remember what Felicity accused you of! He could be stringing you along, hoping you'll lower your guard and let slip something about Tom's whereabouts.'

'Thanks for the gypsy's warning!'

'I mean it, Mickey! Do you want your heart broken all over again?'

'Oh, I don't think there's any danger

of that,' Mickey murmured. 'After what I've been through I'm not likely to rush into anything, am I?'

'And even if you do fancy Jerome, he's only the interim man.'

'What on earth is that?'

'It was in this article I read recently. When you're coming down off an important relationship — say you've been divorced or something — the next person you date is just a sort of stepping stone you use while you get your confidence back. It's never permanent because you carry so much baggage from your previous relationship that you can't see the new one clearly. I suppose it's coloured by what's happened in the past. Once you move on from this interim chap, then you're free to start up something different and lasting.'

'Sounds like a lot of nonsense to me!'

'It's psychology,' Sandie replied, closing her lips firmly.

Mickey supposed it made some sort of sense, but it did little to calm the conflict within her. Her head told her to be sensible, but her heart was a different matter, and there was no way you could control what was in your heart, was there?

Unbeknown to her, Jerome was experiencing similar feelings of ambivalence. What had begun as a slight attraction seemed to be heading in quite another direction, and he wasn't sure that he wanted that. He was thirty years old and so far he had managed to avoid matrimony, although he'd had plenty of relationships with eager young women.

He was in no hurry to settle down, and when the time did come, he was old fashioned enough to want to pledge himself to someone for life. Short term marriages and hasty divorces were not for him.

He thought ruefully that, according to his friends, he had it all. Looks, money, a good education, and a job he loved. But those very advantages often worked against him because he never knew whether a woman was interested in him personally, or in his money.

Mickey was different, as far as he could tell. She didn't ask to be taken to expensive restaurants or nightclubs and she didn't badger him with hints about them having a possible future together. But was she right for him?

On one hand he'd like to shower Mickey with gifts, yet something held him back. He didn't want to try to buy her affections. Again he thought of Felicity, who was always surrounded by a crowd of hangers-on, willing to let her pay for everything because she had the money. Poor little rich girl! The family wealth hadn't done much for her other than attracting hordes of spongers, or conmen like Tom Bowman.

He picked up the phone and punched in Mickey's numbers.

'Hello?'

'Hi, Michaela, it's me, Jerome.'

He hardly needed to identify himself. The sound of his deep voice set her heart racing. She strove to appear nonchalant.

'Hi. What's up?'

'I've been thinking that it's time we got in touch with this Lydia Frew. I want to know if her story checks out. I'm still furious about what this man has done to my sister, but it's this other one I feel sorrier for. I don't know what sort of job she does, if anything, but it must be terrifying to have your retirement savings swept away with no chance of replacing them.'

'I did e-mail her, you know, but I've never had a reply,' Mickey admitted.

'Same here, but probably I can find out more from the police. As she apparently reported her loss to them they should at least be able to tell us where she's living.'

'Do you think they will? Wouldn't that be confidential?'

'Oh, I think that if I explain once again that I'm a solicitor, looking into Felicity's case, they'll cooperate. If that fails, my father is on good terms with the Chief Constable and that should carry some weight. When I find out where Miss Frew is living, I'll make an appointment to see her, and you'd better come with me.'

Mickey replaced the phone, her heart singing, as it always did when she had a date with Jerome to look forward to.

'Are you sure this is it?' Mickey looked up at the house in bewilderment. Surely Lydia Frew didn't live here. It was a beautiful place, set well back from the road, with trees all round. The woman was supposed to have sold her family home and given the proceeds to Tom.

'This is what she told me when we spoke on the phone,' Jerome assured her. However, whatever this house might have been in the past, it was no longer, a one-family unit now, for when they reached the door they found a panel of bells with several names listed underneath, including that of *L. Frew*. Presumably the place was now a warren of bedsits.

Lydia's residence was at the top of the house, a set of attractive rooms tucked under the roof. Mickey guessed they had been servants' quarters at one time. Pleasant enough, with their sloping ceilings and dormer windows, but a bit of a comedown for somebody who had previously owned a house of her own.

At first glance the woman appeared to be older than she had indicated on her website. In her forties, at least, Mickey decided, and so a good few years Tom's senior.

'I'd like to see some identification, please.'

'Certainly, Miss Frew.' Tom pulled out his wallet and handed over his driver's license, as well as a business card which gave his name and that of his firm. Mickey didn't drive, but she was able to produce a photo of herself with Tom, taken in happier days. Lydia drew her lips into a thin line, but she made no comment.

'At least she isn't going to accuse me

of being in on the scam,' Mickey thought, but all the same she resolved to keep quiet and let Jerome do the talking.

'As I've already explained, Miss Frew, I'm interested in this case because my young sister has also been victimised by Bowman. So has Michaela here, up to a point, that is to say Bowman pretended to be in love with her, before leaving her when he met my sister, although she herself wasn't robbed. I've brought her along to hear your story because something you have to say may strike a chord with her, and we need all the help we can get if this man is to be brought to justice.'

Lydia glanced quickly at Mickey before looking down at her own hands, which were twisting in her lap. 'What is it you want to know, Mr Marshall? I've already told my story to the police and when they seemed uninterested I was driven to desperation and spelled it all out on the Internet. I don't know what more I can add.'

'Perhaps you can begin by explaining how you met Bowman, and how exactly he got you to hand over your money to him.'

Lydia's story took a long time in the telling, punctuated by a few sobs and throat clearings. Mickey reflected that it was just as well Jerome wasn't charging her for this consultation, or the bill would have been a large one.

'I seldom got out and about very much towards the end of my parents' lives because they couldn't be left alone for long. They were rather private people and they didn't fancy a neighbour coming in to sit with them, snooping about, as they put it. So after they passed on I joined the golf club here thinking I'd meet new people, and get some fresh air and exercise at the same time.'

'And that is where you met Bowman?'

'That's right. I thought it best to invest in a few lessons with the club professional. We went for coffee after my sessions, and of course he knew that my parents had just died, so he drew me out. He asked me what plans I had for the future. Did I mean to travel, and so on.'

Trying to find out if she was well off, no doubt, Mickey thought.

'I explained that I meant to go back to work, and that I'd have to sell the house, which was far too big for a woman on her own. I'd already moved Mother and Dad downstairs when they started to fail, and the two top floors were shut off. In some ways it was a wrench to think of leaving, after spending so many happy hears there. I was born in that house, you see.'

Jerome nodded sympathetically. Watching him, Mickey would see that he must be good at his job. Instead of barking out questions, as she imagined the police might have done, he listened quietly while the poor woman poured out her story.

'Anyway, the house sold almost as soon as it came on the market, and in fact I did quite well out of it. The prospective buyers were gazumped twice and I ended up with a nice little nest egg for my retirement.'

'And then you chose to come to live here.'

'It was hardly my choice, Mr Marshall. No, at first I stayed with an old school friend while I looked around for a suitable flat for myself.' She blushed suddenly. 'By this time Tom and I were seeing each other on a regular basis, and he kept hinting about us moving in together some day, so I didn't make much of an effort to take on a flat just for one! Phyllis — that's my friend — said there was no hurry. Her husband had been made redundant and she was glad of the bit of money I paid her.'

'And then?'

'When I told Tom about the miserable bit of interest the bank was giving me he said I could do better if I let him invest the money on the stock market. I don't have a clue about that sort of thing, but he seemed to understand it. He told me that my nest egg might seem like a lot now, but with inflation it wouldn't amount to much by the time I was ready to give up work.'

'Now this is very important, Miss Frew. How did you give the money to Bowman?'

She frowned. 'I'm not sure what you mean.'

'Well, was it a lump sum, or in dribs and drabs? Did you give him a cheque, let's say, or perhaps a bank draft?'

'It was just fifty thousand pounds at first. I was a bit nervous about handing over so much money, so I decided to start with that and see how things went.'

Mickey wondered why on earth anyone would hand over large sums of money to a complete stranger, but she knew from tales of woe which occasionally appeared in the newspapers that it happened time and time again. Lydia having just lost both her parents in a short space of time would have felt vulnerable and relished the attention Tom had no doubt lavished on her.

'And how was the cheque made out? To Tom Bowman?'

'Well, no. He had a little investment company — Sunshine Enterprises, he called it. He told me it had something to do with saving tax, and he didn't want me to have to pay out to the government unnecessarily.'

'Moonshine, more like,' Jerome said grimly. 'In other words, he wanted to avoid leaving a paper trail, leading back to him. At the moment I have no idea how he wangled it, but he's probably opened an account under a false name and the police may never be able to catch up with him. He's clever, I'll grant him that. What happened next?'

'Well then he came back and said he'd found a marvellous opportunity, something to do with computers, but he needed more money to invest. Then take the money out of that other stock and use that, I said, but he told me that would be a mistake. It had gone down in value temporarily and I'd be a fool to sell at a loss when I didn't need to.'

'So you gave him more, and, let me guess, he kept coming back with these wonderful opportunities, until he'd bled you dry.'

'Yes and no, Mr Marshall. I did get fifty thousand back.'

Jerome sat up in his chair. 'How on earth did you manage that?'

'By stopping my cheque before he could cash it. I've been offered work at a firm just outside the city, but the bus service isn't very good out in that direction. Unfortunately my car is ancient and none too reliable, so I decided I'd better treat myself to a new one, but I'd need to use some of that money instead of investing it. I'd handed Tom the cheque just a matter of minutes before the personnel officer rang to tell me I'd landed the job, and I thought if I could catch him in time all would be well. I couldn't find him anywhere, so I phoned my bank at once and stopped the cheque.'

'Well done, you!' Jerome clapped his hands together, pleased that something good had come of the whole sorry mess. After advising her to retrieve the cheque from her bank, he said he'd be in touch, and they left.

Mickey felt wrung out by all she had seen and heard, as you do after watching a weepie at the cinema. The difference was that a film usually had a happy ending, and she hoped fervently that such might be the case for Lydia Frew.

'Do you think there's any chance she'll get the rest of her money back?' she asked, as Jerome turned the car in the direction of home.

'Hard to say. It all depends on whether Bowman really bought stocks and shares, or if he's just pocketed the money. At least we'll have that cheque to enter into evidence and that's something. Now, do you want to stop for something to eat, or shall we just head for home?'

9

So how did it go yesterday? Did you find out anything interesting?' It was a sunny Saturday morning, and the two girls were out power walking. They had recently started doing this as a way to keep in shape. Mickey was in reasonable condition, but Sandie felt she herself needed to shed a few pounds. Mickey didn't agree, but as she said, if the walk didn't do them any good, it wouldn't do them any harm.

She shrugged. 'Not really. Jerome took me along in case I picked up on anything Lydia said, but there was nothing new. Oh, except that when Tom took her money, supposedly to invest it, she had to make out the cheques to something called Sunshine Enterprises.'

'Sounds like he was part of a scam, doesn't it?'

'Well, we all know that, don't we!'

'No need to go all sarcastic on me, Mickey Clarke! What I meant was, could he be part of a larger ring? Does he have partners in crime, for instance?'

'I can't answer that. Apparently he told Lydia it had something to do with tax write-offs, but Jerome feels it was just a way to keep his own name out of it.'

Sandie began to puff as they powered their way uphill, and it was a few minutes before she was able to respond to this.

'And what did you think of her, this Lydia Frew? A bit gullible, is she?'

'Oh, I think he moved in on her when she was at her most vulnerable. Her parents had just died, and she was faced with selling their home and finding herself a job. Not easy to do in the best of circumstances, but just then she must have been glad to have someone to lean on. Too bad it had to be a conman.'

'Are you telling me they weren't actually living together, then? That's the way it sounded from what she posted on her website.'

'I think she thought of them as being together because he was talking about them finding a flat together, and he even hinted at marriage. She fell for it, hook, line and sinker. Of course, Tom is very attractive and charming. I should know!' Mickey concluded ruefully.

'At least she got some of her money back in the end and that's more than can be said for Felicity Marshall,' Sandie mused. 'It's funny, you know. I feel sorrier for Lydia than I do for Felicity, yet they probably lost about the same amount of money. The Frews' house probably fetched a tidy sum, wouldn't you say?'

'The difference is that Felicity has everything going for her,' Mickey reminded her friend. 'Wealthy parents, and a home to go to. Lydia has lost all that.'

'Oh, well, let's forget about all this gloomy stuff for a bit; it's too nice a day. Race you to the pillar box! Last one there is a rotten egg!' Sandie dashed off at a great rate, leaving Mickey to tag along behind. She didn't feel like indulging in childish antics. She had other things on her mind.

After leaving Lydia's flat the previous day, she had agreed to have lunch with Jerome, rather than going home right away. This was partly because she was hungry, but also because she wanted to spin out their time together for as long as possible.

The meal they had, and the surroundings in which it was eaten, was as far away from their evening at *The Golden Door* as it was possible to get, but Mickey could not have enjoyed it more.

She was surprised when the car drew up in front of a grimy factory, in a district where it looked as if an expensive car should not be left unattended.

'What's going on? Where are we?'

'Wait and see.' He smiled, turning off the ignition.

He led the way to where a large white caravan was parked, a few yards from the factory gates.

'This may not look like much, but they have the best ham sandwiches in the country! I've stopped here once or twice before, and it's always been well worth the visit.'

As they waited for their coffee he explained that Sam, the owner, made a good living from selling food to the factory workers.

'That's right, love,' the beaming man agreed. 'Of course, some of them brings food from home, but most likes coming to me here. There's nothing like fresh tea and coffee, see. It don't taste the same out of a Thermos. And I try to vary the menu so there's always a nice surprise waiting for them.'

Appetising smells wafted on the air. Chilli con carne seemed to be on offer, as well as the usual chips. 'Better drink up, love,' Sam advised, when Mickey had swallowed the last crumb of her sandwich, licking her fingers to make sure she missed nothing. 'Soon as that hooter goes they'll come pouring out of there and you might get trodden on. Don't say I didn't warn you!'

Back in the car, Mickey watched Jerome out of the corner of her eye. She couldn't quite make him out. She'd had him pegged as the son of a wealthy family, completely at home in places like *The Golden Door*, ordering expensive wines with aplomb. She was seeing a different side of him today. What else was there to know about him?

She soon found out. As they sped through the countryside, with his car purring softly like a contented cat, Jerome turned to her and said something which took her breath away.

'I'm going down to see the parents on Sunday. Want to come along?'

'Er, what?'

He grinned. 'It's all right, they won't eat you! They've heard all about you, of course, because of this Tom Bowman thing.'

'Oh!' and no doubt Felicity has put

her oar in, Mickey thought, so goodness knows what she'll have told them about me!

Jerome seemed to pick up on what she was thinking, for he grinned and said, 'You don't have to worry about anything my sister has said, Michaela. The parents are used to her rambling. Most of it goes in one ear and out the other, believe me.'

'But I don't want to make a bad impression,' she blurted, wishing as soon as the words were out of her mouth that she hadn't said that. It made her look so gauche.

'Oh, they're used to me bringing girls home,' he shrugged, and said no more.

Her ego was instantly deflated. Obviously there was nothing special about this outing to his parents' home, whatever Sandie might read into it.

'But taking you home to meet Mummy and Daddy! It must mean something,' she insisted.

'Apparently not. I'm just the latest in a string of female companions he's taken there, it seems to me.'

'Come on, Mickey. Of course a man of his age must have had numerous girlfriends up to this point; nobody would expect otherwise.' Sandie was about to say that her friend was simply suffering from a lack of confidence after her experiences with Tom, but she thought better of it.

'Are you going to take him up on his offer, then?'

'I said I'd let him know.'

'Oh, Mickey! What have you got to lose? At the very least you'll have a nice drive into the country and probably a slap-up meal when you get there, cooked by some old family retainer. Go on, it'll be a laugh! His old nanny will take you on a tour of the nurseries and show you where young Master Jerome used to sleep. Fascinating stuff. If it was me, I wouldn't miss it for the world.'

Mickey started to laugh. 'All right, I'll go, but I haven't got a thing to wear!'

'Nonsense! You've got a wardrobe full

of stuff, and so have I.'

'But I shan't know what to wear!' Mickey wailed.

'So how is that a problem? It's only for one day! Just ask Jerome what you'll be doing and dress accordingly. They live in the country, don't they? That probably means walking the dogs across a muddy field, so you'll want wellies and heavy pullover.'

'Or it could mean spending the evening at the country club. You can imagine the looks I'd get if I turned up there in boots and an anorak!'

'I imagine our Felicity would lend you one of her cast-offs,' Sandie joked. 'You're about her size, I think!'

Mickey groaned. They probably wore the same size, all right, but put them side by side in similar dresses and there the resemblance would end. Mickey had a nice, slender figure, but Felicity had a much shapelier bosom, and her legs seemed to go on forever. That, plus the self confidence which came of having gone to the best schools, added up to a package which no man could resist.

She mentioned this to Sandie, who sniffed unkindly. 'You're every bit as good as she is, Mickey Clarke! Better, I'd say, with her snooty way of talking to people.'

'It's her nasty tongue I'm afraid of.'

'Nonsense! Stand up for yourself. It's not your fault Tom Bowman led her down the garden path, as my gran used to say. You just give her as good as you get!'

And so, feeling nervous yet intrigued, Mickey accepted Jerome's invitation, and was pleased she had done so when he seemed delighted.

$\star$ $\star$ $\star$

As the car swept around the curved driveway, Mickey waited with interest for her first glimpse of the house where Jerome had spent his childhood. When at last it came into view she didn't know whether to be delighted or disappointed. It was a beautiful Georgian house, but it certainly wasn't like something out of *Brideshead Revisited*.

Throughout the day she realised that, in this day and age, being a millionaire didn't necessarily mean that you could own boats in the Caribbean or a castle in Spain. A sum which, a century ago, would have made you rich beyond the dreams of avarice had greatly deteriorated in value now.

Still, the house was charming enough, with ivy climbing up its rosy brick walls, and tall windows which afforded a fine view of the fields and woods beyond. As the car drew up at the front door four dogs appeared from nowhere, barking joyously.

'Oh, what are they?' Mickey cried, bending down to pat one which was demanding her attention.

'Down, Sam! They're English Setters. Sue over there is the mother and these three are her offspring.'

'But they're not all the same colour,' Mickey said, still fondling the black ears of the tallest dog. 'Did Sue have a fling with another sort of breed?'

'Better not let Mother hear you say that!' Jerome laughed. 'No, English Setters do come in different colours. Sam there is what is known as a Blue Belton and these others are Orange Belton.'

He pointed to two eager animals whose cheerful freckled faces were brown and white. Mickey felt foolish, and resolved not to let her nervousness trick her into making silly remarks.

'Come on, let's get you inside. Mother will have heard the dogs barking and be wondering where we've got to.'

'So you must be Michaela.' Julia Marshall smiled. 'I've heard all about you from the children. Please excuse me if I don't get up. I've been gardening since seven o'clock this morning and I'm absolutely exhausted. And sit down, do. I'll get a crick in my neck looking up at you like this.'

Once again, Mickey's preconceived notions did a right-about turn. Where was the stately woman with the pearls and the expensive hairdo? Jerome's mother was wearing faded corduroys and an old jumper with patched elbows. Thick socks covered her feet, which were propped up on an oaken coffee table.

The dogs had followed them into the room and had now flopped into every available couch and armchair. There was nowhere for Mickey to sit until Jerome ordered Sam to remove himself to the hearth rug. It was all very relaxed and homelike. She leaned back, letting the conversation flow over her, as mother and son chatted together.

'Where's Dad?'

'Gone down to the village for his newspapers. He told me to say that if Michaela would care for a tour of the estate, he'll be glad to show her around. Or perhaps you have other plans for the day?'

'Not really. You know me; I just like to loaf around after the hurly burly of office life.'

'I daresay, but won't that be a bit boring for your friend? Would you like to see the house, Michaela?'

Mickey admitted that she would, so she obediently trotted after Jerome as they peered into one room after another. There were no old retainers in sight and she wondered who looked after all this.

'Oh, a woman comes in from the village two days a week, and we have a gardener who does the heavy work outside, but that's about it. The parents manage the rest of it.' He looked amused. 'Why, did you expect to find a flock of servants with bedrooms in the attics?'

She blushed. Her imagination hadn't taken her quite that far, but she had expected to find the Marshalls living in the lap of luxury. Now it appeared that they were normal people who just happened to have more money than the rest of us. Felicity's snooty behaviour had led her to believe something different.

At that moment Felicity appeared out of nowhere, as if thinking about her could cause her to arrive in a puff of smoke.

'What on earth are you doing here?' she demanded, looking down her nose at Mickey.

'Charming!' Jerome sniffed. 'You remember my little sister, I suppose?'

'How could I forget?' Mickey muttered, and immediately battle lines were drawn.

As soon as the words were out of her mouth she regretted having said them; after all she was a guest in their family home. However, she was determined not to let the other girl put her down. Just because she was rich it didn't mean she was better than other people!

Jerome didn't seem to have noticed anything amiss. 'Come to that, what are you doing here, Fliss? I thought you were on the Continent?'

Her sister shrugged. 'Everybody had to get back to work. Too boring! I couldn't be bothered staying on alone,

119

so I came home.'

'You mean you've moved back in with the parents?'

'Where else should I go, just tell me that! Her boyfriend has taken all my money, hasn't he! And Dad's no better. He's been going on about me training for a job or something. I ask you! Can you see me working in a potty little office, or carrying bedpans in some grotty hospital?'

Jerome laughed, but Mickey looked away. No, Felicity was one of life's butterflies. She wouldn't last five minutes in their office with Miss Phipps in charge, and as for doing something to help those in need, she was just too selfish. Having a moneyed background had done absolutely nothing for that young woman's character.

★   ★   ★

'And this is my room,' Jerome announced, flinging open a door at the end of a long hall. 'At least it was, when I was growing up. These days it's only used when I stay overnight, of course.'

Charmed to get a glimpse of the boy he had been, Mickey stepped inside, looking at the bookcase, with its rows of volumes by Arthur Ransome and Enid Blyton, and the shelf of model cars. There was even a battered teddy on the bedside table. Her lips curved in a smile as she saw all this.

Behind her, Felicity attempted to put the knife in. 'A bit different from his flat, wouldn't you say, Michelle? Of course you'll have seen that, he takes all his women there.'

'Run along and play, Flissie.' Jerome laughed. 'Three's a crowd, or haven't you heard?'

His sister flounced off, much to Mickey's relief. Jerome obviously didn't take her seriously, so that was all that mattered.

Gerald Marshall, when he finally returned home, was an older version of his son, with the same sort of manner — quiet but firm. Mickey soon felt at ease with him and when Felicity announced she was going riding, the house suddenly seemed more pleasant and she settled down to enjoy her visit there.

The day passed all too quickly and when dinner was over Jerome announced that they should be heading back to town. 'Monday morning comes early, you know.'

'Thank you for having me, Mrs Marshall,' Mickey said, as they were leaving. 'I've had a lovely time, and that roast chicken was delicious.'

'I'm glad you've enjoyed yourself, Michaela. You must come and see us again. Jerome, dear, you simply must bring her to watch the sheepdog trials. Your father is letting them use the top field this year, so it'll be such fun, having it happen right on our doorstep.'

'Yes, Mother. I'd like to see that myself. Now, we really must get off.'

'Goodbye, dear!'

★ ★ ★

It was over. Mickey had met Jerome's parents, and been accepted by them. She had seen him in his own milieu. She had even survived his sister's machinations. Now all that remained was to see if he approved of the way she had fitted into his own setting.

Her own mother had said that taking a boyfriend home to meet parents was a two-way street. Seeing him against your own background was a true test of how well matched the two of you were.

If that was the case it certainly hadn't worked with Tom Bowman! The Clarkes had welcomed him with open arms, describing him as 'a very nice young man.' How wrong they had been!

'Why so quiet?' Jerome asked.

'Just thinking about everything, that's all.'

'Tom, you mean?'

'Partly.'

'It's time to forget all that, Michaela. It's time to move on. Believe me, there are better things waiting around the corner.'

Was he speaking generally, or was he hinting that they might be taking their relationship to another level? She couldn't tell, and as he said nothing more she was left up in the air and feeling rather bewildered.

10

Mickey! Where on earth have you been? I've been trying to get hold of you all day!'

'There's nothing wrong, is there, Mum? Nothing's happened to Dad, has it?'

'Of course not! What makes you ask that?'

'It's just that it's a funny time to be calling. And I haven't been answering because Jerome took me down to the country to meet his parents.'

'Never mind all that, you're here now. You'll never guess what's happened over here, Mickey. It's come right out of the blue.'

Mickey forced herself to stay calm. She knew her mother of old. No doubt she'd get to the point in due course. As long as everyone was in good health, that was all that mattered.

'I've seen Tom Bowman!' Joyce announced triumphantly. 'There! What do you think of that?'

'You've seen Tom?' Mickey echoed. 'But how? You can't have, Mum. You've seen someone who looks like him, that's all.'

'Oh, no, dear; it was definitely him. It was in a big shopping precinct. I'd gone there to start my Christmas shopping; it's early, I know, but parcels for overseas have to go off at the end of October, which doesn't leave me much time. Well, I stopped to window-shop outside a men's clothing store and there he was! Standing at the counter inside, paying for something or other, bold as brass!'

'Did you go and speak to him?'

'No, I didn't, Mickey. I'm not that stupid. If he'd recognised me he'd have run a mile, and that would have been the last anyone would have seen of him. No, I followed him at a discreet distance and when he went into a café and sat down I knew he'd be there for a bit, so I called the police.'

'Good for you. And they believed you? I can't imagine what you told them.'

Joyce cleared her throat. Mickey thought her mother seemed embarrassed.

'Well, I suppose I must have sounded hysterical, but I was a bit worked up, it was all so unexpected. I said I was keeping an eye on a man who'd stolen a lot of money and they somehow got the idea that I'd been mugged. They came rushing in and put Tom in handcuffs, and people were screaming and rushing out of the place, just like you see in the movies.

'Off we went, with him insisting it was all a mistake and he'd done nothing, and the police asking me if I thought I needed to see a doctor. It was quite a scene, I can tell you.'

'And it really was Tom?'

'I've told you that, haven't I?'

'I know but, it seems so incredible. For all we knew he might be anywhere in the world but he turns up right under your nose. That's a pretty big coincidence, Mum.'

'Coincidences do happen, but you're right. The police were sceptical at first, especially when Tom kept insisting that he didn't know me, and unfortunately he did have identification in a completely different name.

'They said they understood that my daughter had been taken in by a conman, and my feelings about that must have upset me to the point where I'd accused a complete stranger of being responsible.'

'Ouch!'

'Yes, that was upsetting, but then luckily I remembered the address of that website where Lydia Frew told her story. I insisted they look it up, which they did, and after that they apologised for not taking me seriously. As they said, it might still be a coincidence, someone else who looks like him, but at least they're keeping him in custody until they investigate his background.

He's calling himself Todd Bowles now.'

'That's great, Mum. But I don't understand why he'd go to Canberra, of all places. He knew perfectly well that you and Dad would be there. I know it's a big city, being the capital and all that, but even so, he must have known there was a risk of coming across you at some point. I wouldn't have thought he'd be that much of an idiot.'

'Oh, but I'm not in Canberra just now, Mickey. That just shows you how upset this whole thing has made me. No, I'm in Sydney. I'm calling you from my hotel.'

'Sydney! What are you doing there?'

'I'm here on a coach tour with some of the university wives. Among other things we've been taking in a special exhibit at the Museum of Contemporary Art. Someone I've got to know here invited me to come along when one of the other ladies had to drop out. I wasn't interested at first — Canberra has good galleries if I want to look at paintings — but your Dad said I might as well go and take a look at Sydney while I have the chance. Once we come back to England we may never get back to Australia again.'

'Let me get this straight. You ran into Tom when you were in a shopping precinct in Sydney.'

'Isn't that what I just said? A person can only look at so many pictures in one day, you know. We're allowed plenty of time to fit in a little shopping as well!'

Mickey's head was in a whirl by the time she put down the receiver. What with the excitement of the day, and now this.

There was no way she could calm herself down enough to get to sleep. She tried a warm bath, hot milk, and soft music. Nothing worked. She got up again at three o'clock and tried reading for a while. Then she lay down again, only to toss and turn until she finally fell asleep about four a.m.

★ ★ ★

The shrill sound of her alarm clock shocked her into wakefulness three hours later. Monday morning! What a way to start off the work week.

The one good thing about all this was that Miss Phipps was missing from the office when Mickey arrived.

'What happened to you?' Sandie yelped. 'You look like death warmed over.'

'Thanks very much! I need a coffee. Where's Phippsie?'

'She called in sick. Apparently she's come down with her annual cold, and she doesn't want to spread it round the office. You haven't caught it too, have you?'

'I hope not. I've got enough on my plate without that.'

Sandie's eyes opened wide. 'Come on, then, what happened yesterday? Did you like the Marshalls? More to the point, did they like you?'

'Oh, that went fine.'

'That sounds suspiciously like damning with faint praise to me.'

Mickey sat down at her desk, cradling her coffee mug between her cold hands.

'Everything was fine, honestly. I'll tell you more about it later, OK? What's happened is, I had a phone call from Mum which got me all worked up, and I had trouble falling asleep afterwards. She went to Sydney with friends, and while she was there she spotted Tom, swanning around a shopping precinct as cool as you please!'

'I don't believe it!'

'It's quite true, and what's more she called the police while he was sitting in a café having lunch, and they came and nabbed him!'

Sandie clapped her hands together with glee. 'That's great! Now that rotten beast will get what's coming to him! I wouldn't like to be in his shoes when he ends up in court and has to face the woman he robbed. I bet Jerome is pleased about this, isn't he?'

Mickey punched herself on the forehead. 'I haven't even thought about

Jerome,' she groaned. 'Three hours sleep doesn't do much for the old brain cells.'

'Then don't you think you'd better call him at once?' Sandie demanded. 'Really, Mickey, this is news he'll want to hear, and I'm sure Lydia Frew will be delighted about this as well. What are you waiting for? Pick up that phone!'

★ ★ ★

Jerome was indeed pleased when he heard what Mickey had to tell him.

'I'll get on to our police at once,' he told her. 'I'm sure the Australian police are quite capable, but it won't do any harm for their British counterparts to be in touch. I expect they have plenty of crime to take care of in their own city, without worrying about a minor fraud in another country. It will also give the authorities here a head start on investigating Tom's change of identity. He's going under the name of Todd

Bowles, you said?'

'I'm sure you'll do as you think best,' Mickey countered, stifling a yawn. 'There's no rush, though, is there? After what he's done he deserves to cool his heels in a cell for a bit. It'll be good practice for when he eventually gets sent down, which I trust will be for a long time.'

'There is every need to act as quickly as possible,' Jerome said. 'I'm not sure how the law works over there, but I suspect that if we're not careful he might be let out on bail, and before you know it he could do the disappearing trick again.'

'Oh, but surely they'd take his passport away before they let him go.'

'Very likely, but don't forget, Mickey, this man has plenty of cash stashed away somewhere. If he was able to get one forged passport he could certainly get another. The worst case scenario would be that he'd simply skip town and disappear somewhere, just another foreign tourist travelling around. They'd catch up with him eventually, I suppose, but it could take forever, and in the meanwhile whatever money he still has would be frittered away.'

'Yes, I see.' Mickey felt rather gloomy at the thought.

'Are you still there? Look, I'm grateful to your mother for letting us know about this, and if you hear from her again, will you let me know what she says?'

'Of course.'

'Right then, I must get on. Have a good day.' He rang off.

★　★　★

'I just don't know where I stand with Jerome,' Mickey complained.

'I don't know what you mean,' Sandie countered. 'He's taken you to the best restaurant in town, and he's introduced you to his parents. I'd say the two of you certainly have something going.'

'Yes, but are we officially an item? It's

all one-sided. I wait for him to invite me out, and I go along with it, but when does he ask me what I'd like to do?'

'No problem there. Just come up with something and ask if he'd like to join you.'

Mickey pulled a face. 'I suppose you mean that old dodge where I say I've been given two tickets for a concert by somebody who can't go, and would he like to help me use them?'

'You're not living in the real world, Mickey Clarke! Hasn't anyone ever told you that men and women are equals now? Ask him to your flat for a meal. If you're afraid he might get the wrong idea — bold hussy and all that — invite me and Brendan as well.'

'I suppose I could.'

'Your enthusiasm is underwhelming!' Sandie groaned.

Mickey promised to think about it, but before she could bring herself to the point, Jerome got there first.

'I'm phoning to invite you to come as

my guest to the Golf Club annual dinner dance. How are you fixed for the sixteenth?'

'I didn't know you were a member there,' she remarked.

'Oh, absolutely. I haven't had a game in an age, due to the pressure of work, but I'm still in good standing.'

She wasn't sure if she could face it. Unhappy memories came flooding back, and she worried that people would size her up as the former girlfriend of the conman golf pro.

However, she had done nothing to be ashamed of, so why shouldn't she go? Making up her mind, she said she'd be happy to accept his invitation.

★ ★ ★

'Will you be going, Sandie?' she asked, having recalled that Brendan was a member. It would be lovely if the four of them could share a table at the event. But Sandie shook her head ruefully.

'I'm afraid we're not in that league,

not at one hundred pounds a plate! If I had that kind of money I can think of umpteen things I'd rather do with it.'

'Whew, really? I'm not sure if I approve, either, but when people are starving in Third World countries.'

'Then send a donation to the Red Cross and let the golfers get on with it. You're not responsible for what other people do with their money.'

Now came the age-old problem. What to wear! By raiding both their wardrobes Mickey had managed to outfit herself for her evening at *The Golden Door*, but the Golf Club do was something else entirely.

The women would be wearing designer gowns and she would completely be outclassed in anything she could find in the High Street shops.

Those same women were probably the type who wore such garments only once, so even if she did find something which might do, it would be a waste of money. If she continued to see Jerome she couldn't use it again.

'Then hire something!' Sandie insisted. 'There's a very good shop where you can hire evening dress and wedding garments. A lot of people are in your position, Mickey. They want to look their best for some special occasion, without breaking the bank. How about it?'

It sounded like the perfect solution, and the following Saturday the two girls set off to see what they could find.

However, when they turned the corner on to Market Street, where the place was located, they came to a sudden stop in front of a charity shop.

There in the window, displayed on a plaster mannequin, was the most gorgeous dress Mickey had ever seen. A soft, pale turquoise, it was made from what appeared to be satin, overlaid with toning chiffon.

The fitted bodice was held up with narrow straps. It was the sort of dress that looks perfectly plain when seen hanging up, but which would be absolutely stunning when worn.

'Just look at that!' Sandie breathed. 'I

bet it's just your size. Shall we go in and take a closer look?'

Sure enough, it was the right size, and even more wonderful was the fact that it fell within Mikey's price range. It even had a matching evening bag, without a mark on it.

'Who on earth would want to discard a beautiful gown like this?' she wondered, but the woman in charge didn't know.

'I expect the owner fell pregnant and couldn't fit into it any more, or something like that. Shall I wrap it for you, dear?'

So after that it was simply a question of finding the right shoes and deciding what jewellery to wear.

Naturally Mickey owned nothing that could compare with the real gems that the wealthier women probably had access to, but at least she had youth and beauty on her side. According to Sandie, anyway!

★ ★ ★

When they arrived at the Golf Club on the appointed evening, Mickey was keyed up with anticipation. There was the meal to enjoy, followed by the usual speeches which had to be sat through, and after that, the dance.

There was to be a full orchestra, and she looked forward to drifting around in Jerome's arms as the evening wore on, although he warned her that there would be some more energetic dances first, in deference to the younger set.

'Aren't we the younger set, then?' she teased. A considerable number of grey-haired guests were already circulating with drinks in their hands, and surely there would be more sedate music for them to enjoy.

'Oh, you know what I mean.' He grinned, waving a hand in the direction of a laughing group of junior members. 'Come along, I must introduce you to my aunt and uncle. Aunt Rosalind has spotted us and is signalling to me.'

These were the Smythes, of course. Mickey had heard of them from

Brendan, when Tom's relationship with Felicity had first been suspected.

They greeted Mickey pleasantly as Jerome performed the introductions, and Quentin, the husband, went off to fetch her a drink.

'Where is Felicity this evening, dear?' Rosalind Smythe asked. 'We could have picked her up at her flat, only we thought she'd be coming with you.'

Mickey's heart sank. She could have done without Felicity's presence this evening. She had to remind herself that this was the other girl's milieu while she herself was merely an invited guest.

'I think she's found herself a new beau, Aunt,' Jerome told her.

'Is that so? Then let us hope that he's a better type than the scumbag she fell for the last time.'

Mickey's eyes opened wide, but Rosalind Smythe seemed completely unaware of her gaffe. Obviously she didn't know, or had forgotten, about Mickey's own relationship to Tom Bowman. Jerome shot her a concerned look, but she managed a reassuring smile and he looked relieved.

'If you'll excuse me, I must go and have a word with Mabel Bosanquet over there.' Rosalind smiled, putting her glass down on a nearby table. 'I'll see you again later, my dears, and I know that Quentin will want a dance with this lovely young lady!'

'I'm afraid we turned up a bit too early,' Jerome said. 'Nothing much is happening yet. Would you like to step out on to the terrace? The view from there is rather splendid.'

The view was indeed lovely, stretching out over the beautifully kept links to the woods beyond. Below the terrace itself there were flower borders filled with colourful perennials, and trees from which strings of silver lights dangled. The whole scene gave the effect of a fairy tale garden.

Unfortunately a sharp breeze blew up, and although Mickey was quite prepared to put up with the chill, Jerome insisted that they go back indoors. Catching sight of herself in the glass doors she excused herself to go to the loo, saying she wanted to tidy her hair.

Rosalind and her friend, Mabel, were already standing in front of the long mirror, repairing their make-up, when the door to one of the cubicles opened and Felicity Marshall stepped out. She stopped short when she saw Mickey, and immediately burst out laughing.

'I don't believe it! You're wearing my dress!'

Her aunt looked up, puzzled.

'What are you trying to say, dear?'

'Oh, what a hoot, Auntie! She's come here with poor Jerry, wearing my cast-offs! That's the dress I bought for the hunt ball. I was sick of it, so I donated it to the charity shop, and I suppose that's where she found it! Oh, Cinderella, you shall go to the ball!'

'Really, Felicity!' Rosalind snapped. 'How could you be so unkind? Your mother would be so ashamed of you if she could hear this.'

Felicity tossed her head. She cast a triumphant look at Mickey whose hard won confidence suddenly deserted her. She should never have come, she could see that now. With a sob she turned and ran out of the room, and out into the night. And she had no glass slipper to leave behind, and no Prince Charming to come in search of her.

11

Afterwards, Mickey was never quite sure how she made it home. She had no idea where to find a bus stop, and if she had found one, she would have looked ridiculous climbing on board the way she was dressed. The club was at the end of a long, winding country road a long way from the centre of town and it was too far for her to walk home in flimsy, high-heeled sandals.

'Cab, miss?'

A taxi had drawn up beside her, having just left a couple of revellers at the main entrance. Had she enough money in her bag? Possibly, if she didn't give too large a tip. It was beginning to rain now, and her hair was plastered on to her head. Gratefully, she climbed inside the car.

'Where to, love?'

Mickey gave her address, feeling

honour bound to tell the driver that she might not have enough money to travel the whole way and he might have to let her out before they arrived. He was an elderly man with daughters of his own, and he assured her that he'd see her to her door, even if she had to call at the garage the next day with the balance of the fare.

'Boyfriend let you down, has he?'

'Something like that,' she sniffed. If only it were that simple!

She managed to hold back the tears until she reached home, chilled to the marrow. Then, clad in flannel pyjamas, with her head wrapped in a towel, she sank down in an armchair and began to sob, calling herself every sort of idiot.

Of course her encounter with Felicity had been a shock, but need she have responded like a child facing a bully in the school playground? A more sophisticated person would have laughed it off, or thought up a witty response, but not Mickey Clarke! If she had any sort of backbone she'd have ignored Felicity and carried on, but no, she had run away.

She could at least have made some excuse to Jerome, saying she had a headache, perhaps, and needed to go lie down. As it was she had left him to wonder where she'd disappeared to, which was rude, if nothing else.

And she had left the way wide open for Felicity to spin him a yarn which would turn him off Mickey completely. It wasn't only her lovely evening which had been ruined; it had probably put paid to their relationship as well.

Fortunately for her, Rosalind Smythe had put two and two together and decided to take charge. Having no children of her own, she thought of Felicity as the daughter she'd never had, but no daughter of hers would dare to behave like that and get away with it, she told herself.

Julia had spoiled the girl, and now they were reaping a bitter harvest.

The money the girl had thrown away on that wicked young man was bad enough. The fact that she was selfish and unpleasant was worse. If she went through life doing that sort of thing, she'd never find lasting happiness, of that Rosalind was sure.

'Have you seen Michaela?' Jerome asked, as his aunt appeared at his side. 'She said she was just going to tidy her hair, but she's been gone a long time.'

'I'm afraid there's been a bit of a scene,' Rosalind murmured. 'Felicity happened to be there when your friend walked in, and the little madam made a few nasty remarks which caused some distress. Michaela ran out before I could stop her, and I think she must have left the building.'

Exasperated, Jerome leaned back and closed his eyes. 'Now why on earth would she do that? I know that Felicity has her moments, but Michaela is a grown woman. Surely she could have stood up for herself! Why didn't she come to me and explain what had happened?'

Now it was his aunt's turn to look exasperated. Men! Would she ever understand them?

'Listen carefully, my boy! Felicity is your sister.'

'What about it?'

'No well brought up young woman is going to come to you and tell tales about a member of your family, Jerry. Quite apart from the fact that it just isn't cricket, she'd hesitate because she didn't want to put your back up. Surely you can see that.'

'I suppose so.'

'You suppose so! Meanwhile, your guest has run off into the night having been insulted by your sister. What do you propose to do about it? The least you can do is to go after her and make sure she's reached home safely.'

He got up, muttering something rude under his breath, although whether he was complaining about Mickey, Felicity, Rosalind, or all three was anyone's guess. Well, she had done the best she could. It was in his hands now. Sighing, Rosalind went in search of her husband.

Mickey had stopped shaking at last, and was debating whether to go to bed when the doorbell rang. 'Who is it?'

'Jerome. Let me in, please.' His disembodied voice came up through the intercom.

'Go away. I don't want to see you.'

'Then I'll huff, and I'll puff, and I'll blow your house down!'

The quotation from the old fairy tale was so unexpected, coming from Jerome Marshall, that Mickey was forced to laugh.

'Oh, all right, then, but you can't stay long.'

Jerome came into the flat, shaking the water off his raincoat as he came. One quick glance around the room told him everything he needed to know. The pretty dress, ruined and water stained, was flung over the back of a chair. Mickey's sandals were lying in a corner and it was obvious that they were unfit for further wear. One of the straps had pulled loose from the sole during her headlong flight across the Golf Club parking lot.

Mickey herself was equally bedraggled. She was cuddled up in a chenille bathrobe which was faded and worn, and her hair was hanging in rats' tails because she hadn't had the energy to use her hair drier on it. Jerome was suddenly overcome with a wave of tenderness for her.

'Do you mind if I sit down?'

She shook her head.

'Is that a yes or a no?'

'Sit there if you want, but I have nothing to say.'

'But I do, Michaela. I want you to know that I'd planned to ask you to marry me tonight. Oh, blow, this is coming out all pear-shaped. I mean I was going to pop the question at the dance, not that I wanted you to go to the altar this evening!'

Mickey stared at him dumbly. Was he about to tell her that he'd been saved from making a dreadful mistake, having seen what a spineless idiot she was? But no; he was gazing at her tenderly.

'On the way here I thought we could still save the situation,' he went on. 'I could take you back to the club and we'd take up where we left off. However, I can see that your clothes are a bit worse for wear.'

'I'll never wear that frock again!' Mickey shuddered. 'I'll get it cleaned and send it back to the charity shop, that's if it isn't completely ruined. Rain doesn't do much for chiffon, I'm afraid.'

He wasn't sure what that was all about, but he went on to suggest that as neither of them had eaten anything they should have a takeaway delivered.

'Two hundred pounds down the drain!' Mickey mourned. 'Can you ever forgive me for rushing off before we'd even eaten?'

'It's only money. Besides, most of it counts as a donation, so it's tax deductible. That's the least of my worries. Now then, curry or Chinese?'

'Not curry, I'll never get the smell out of the flat.'

'Right, then, Chinese it is.'

As she had said to Sandie on a day which seemed a hundred years ago, Mickey was never quite sure what was going on in Jerome's head. Only a moment ago he'd told her of his intention to propose to her at the dance. Now he was talking about food!

He hadn't stormed out of the flat, saying it was all over between them, so was he still thinking of marrying her? Or was he merely playing for time? There was only one way to find out, and she had to stop being such a wimp!

'Did you mean what you said just now, about wanting to marry me?'

He frowned. 'Yes, of course, but I can't propose now, can I? Not unless you have something else to put on and we try to get back before the orchestra packs up for the night. My idea was we'd be circling the floor to some dreamy music, and I'd whisper sweet nothings in your ear before steering you to some private spot where I'd go down on one knee. I was thinking of the terrace, before the rain started to pelt down.'

'I don't need to be at the golf club for that.' Mickey smiled.

'But a woman needs a romantic setting when her future husband proposes!'

'Men!' Mickey laughed. 'You don't understand anything!'

'That's what Aunt Rosalind said,' he replied, before sweeping her into his arms.

★　★　★

One result of the evening was that Mickey caught a streaming cold. Sandie disputed this. 'Colds are caused by a virus,' she insisted, when she arrived at the flat bearing two cans of chicken soup and a bunch of bananas. 'You've got this cold because it's doing the rounds of the office. I expect I'll have it next. Now, I want you to tell me all about the Golf Club do. I'm dying to know how it went.'

'If you must know, it was a complete and utter disaster.' Mickey sniffed, blowing her nose violently.

'Oh, no! What on earth happened?'

'Felicity is what happened. It turns out that my lovely dress had belonged to her, before she got sick of it! She lost no time in rubbing my nose in it, in front of everyone there. Well, I'm exaggerating a bit, it was only two women in the ladies' loo, but one of them happened to be Jerome's aunt'

'I can't believe it! I trust you gave her as good as you got.'

'Actually, no. I was so humiliated, Sandie! All I wanted to do was to get out of there as quickly as possible. I ran outside and luckily found a taxi and came home.'

Sandie's hand flew to her mouth. 'And what about Jerome? Did you just leave him sitting there, wondering where you'd gone?'

'I'm afraid so.'

Sandie grimaced. 'I suppose that's it, then. Goodbye to the great romance! I'm sorry it's happened, but at least you won't have to put up with that awful Felicity any more.'

'I don't know about that, but you see, Jerome didn't just sit there. He followed me here and he wasn't angry at all. In fact, he's asked me to marry him!'

'Don't keep me in suspense! Did you say yes?' Sandie squealed.

'Let me put it this way,' Mickey smiled, 'how are you fixed for being a bridesmaid at a Christmas wedding?'

While Sandie was laughing and exclaiming the phone rang. It was Mickey's mother, calling from Australia.

'I'll pop back tomorrow!' Sandie mouthed, heading for the door when she realised that it was likely to be a long conversation.

'Who was that, dear?' Joyce asked, having heard the door close. 'I hope I didn't interrupt anything.'

'Just Sandie, Mum. Are you back in

Canberra now?'

'Yes, that's why I'm calling, just to let you know. Otherwise, there's no particular news. Your father is well, but you sound a bit stuffed up. Are you all right?'

'It's just a cold. I think I caught it at the office. But listen, Mum, I've something to tell you both. I was just waiting until you got back from Sydney.'

'There's nothing wrong, is there?' Joyce sounded anxious. What with one thing and another things hadn't gone well for Mickey in the past few months, and she hoped that her daughter wasn't having a streak of bad luck.

'Everything is fine, Mum! In fact, it's just wonderful. Jerome Marshall has asked me to marry him, and I've said yes.'

Mickey could hear excited noises at the other end of the line. That was Joyce, calling her husband to the phone, wanting him to share the good news.

'Congratulations, old girl,' Joe Clarke

boomed. 'Well done! You must let us know what your plans are, so we can get on the job. It's not every day that our only daughter ties the knot!'

'We were thinking of a Christmas wedding, Dad. I know that's only a few months away, but we have no reason to wait.'

'Oh, but we won't be back in England by then,' Joyce wailed.

In all the excitement that fact hadn't occurred to Mickey. Of course her parents would want to see her wedding, and she certainly wanted them there as well.

'It's OK, Mum. Nothing is settled yet. This is all very new, you understand. We haven't really got past the stage of accepting the fact that we really mean to get married.'

'I hope you're not rushing into things,' Joyce cautioned. 'I know what it's like to be so much in love that you can't bear the thought of being separated from the other person. It's just that it doesn't seem long since you were head over heels in love with that Tom chap, and now you're planning to commit yourself for the rest of your life to Jerome Marshall. Don't you think you could be on the rebound?'

'No, Mum. This isn't the same thing at all. Now I've met Jerome I know what real love is. Tom was just a sort of stepping stone on the way to the real thing.'

Joe Clarke cut in now. 'Is there any particular reason why you fancy a Christmas wedding?'

'I don't know, Dad. In my mind it all seems so special. The music, the decorations, the lights everywhere . . . '

'All just external trappings, love. Just take all this one step at a time, will you?'

'Of course, Dad, and I will keep you in the picture. When I've discussed everything with Jerome I'll get back to you both. You can count on that.'

'And that's another thing,' he interrupted. 'This chap of yours; when do we get to meet him? I trust you're going to want my approval, especially considering what went on before with Tom! And what about his family? Are they a decent sort of people?'

'The Marshalls are lovely, Dad. They've made me feel very welcome.'

'That's all right then. Well, we'll wait to hear from you, love.'

'And think about what I've said,' Joyce murmured, as the receiver went down.

* * *

Mickey was disappointed that her parents hadn't shown more enthusiasm. She felt so happy herself that it was hard for her to understand why other people might not feel the same way.

Jerome had seemed so loving and protective, and if he could propose marriage to her when she was looking like a hag, it showed that he really cared about her. She smiled, remembering that he'd told her how he'd fallen in love with her at first sight, when he had brought his sister to this very flat, trying to get to the bottom of Tom's disappearance. He had felt then that she was transparently honest and that it had been impossible to imagine that she could be in league with Bowman.

Mickey had wanted a Christmas wedding ever since she was a little girl, making outfits for her Barbie dolls. Her dress would be made from heavy white satin, with white faux fur trim at the wrists and neck. Her bridesmaid, whoever she was, would wear a floor-length gown of dark green velvet. The church would be decorated with red and white poinsettias. She could see it all now.

Tom had gone along with her dream. Not that he cared about bridal outfits, but he liked the idea of a honeymoon in Australia, where the Christmas holidays took place in the middle of summer.

It was funny that it had never occurred to either of them that if the wedding took place in England, the Clarkes would still be in Australia at the time. Perhaps that was the problem; it was all a dream. Now she was experiencing real life.

'I can see the difficulty,' Jerome remarked, when appealed to. 'Of course your parents must be at the wedding. Why can't they just fly over for it and travel back with us afterwards?'

'Because that would cost money, Jerome, money they can't afford.'

'We could pay their way, couldn't we?'

'Dad is a proud man. He would never go for that!'

'No, perhaps not. Then why don't we get married over there? I'm sure it could be arranged, although there would probably have to be some sort of waiting period, to establish residency.'

'That might be OK for your parents and their friends, but I have family members who simply have to be invited, and then there's Sandie. I want her for my bridesmaid. No, the wedding must take place here in England.'

It seemed they had reached an

impasse. Meanwhile, the Marshalls were delighted when they heard the news of their son's engagement. They agreed that, as parents of the bride, the Clarkes had the right to take charge of the wedding, but they offered to throw an engagement party as their contribution to the couple's happiness.

'That's very kind of you, but could that wait for a bit?' Mickey said gingerly. 'I'm still a bit under the weather from this cold, and I need to be at my best if I'm meeting new people.' She and Jerome exchanged glances. He understood what was behind this — she needed time to recover from the debacle of the Golf Club dinner dance.

'Just as you wish, dear,' Julia said, 'but may I offer you one piece of advice? If the wedding is to take place in England I suggest you book the church right away or you may lose out. I'm sure that Christmas is a busy time for weddings, not to mention all the other rituals of the season.'

Mickey was just concluding that her

future mother-in-law was a sensible person, when Julia spoke up again. 'You must decide on whom you'd like to ask to be your best man, Jerry. Perhaps one of the other partners in your law firm? And Michaela, dear, I'm sure Felicity would just adore to be your bridesmaid.'

Over my dead body, Mickey thought. It was time to nip this one in the bud!

'I'm sorry,' she said firmly, but I'm having just one bridesmaid, and that will be my best friend, Alexandra Lomax.'

'Of course, that's for you to decide,' Julia said sweetly, and the battle was won.

12

The buzzer sounded at Mickey's flat. She wasn't expecting anyone, and while she would have been glad to see Jerome, she rather hoped it was someone else. She was catching up on some housekeeping tasks and was wearing her oldest jeans and a pair of fuzzy slippers.

'Mum! Where did you spring from?' Amazed, she peered down into the stairwell. 'Where's Dad? Isn't he with you?'

'Just let me get inside the door, will you, before you start peppering me with questions! And put the kettle on, do. I'm parched. That's all I could think of all the way in from the airport, a nice cup of tea!'

Mickey made a pot of tea as quickly as possible. Her mother certainly had some explaining to do!

'It's quite simple,' Joyce Clarke explained, when she had swallowed two scalding cups of tea in quick succession. 'Your father and I talked it over, and we decided that I should come to England and mastermind the arrangements for your wedding. He can't leave the university just now, but he'll pop over in time for the big day. All right?'

'All right? It's wonderful, Mum! But the expense! Have you had to borrow from the bank for this?'

Joyce smiled. 'No need to worry. Many years ago your father and I started a little fund to pay for our only daughter's wedding, whenever that day came. It's grown to quite a substantial amount over the years, and we decided we should use some of it to pay our fares to come to England. It may mean that we have to keep the guest list a bit shorter than we would have liked, but one can't have everything in this life.'

'Oh, Mum, I'm so happy to see you! And of course having you and Dad there on my big day means the world to me. I wouldn't care if we had no guests at all!'

'What about the Marshalls, though?' Joyce bit her lip. 'You say they're wealthy people. They're bound to have all sorts of friends they want to invite.'

'I'm sure we can work something out, Mum. It's what the bride's parents say that goes when it comes to planning a wedding.'

As it happened, the Marshalls were happy to cooperate. Jerome drove Mickey and her mother to his old family home, where they received a gracious welcome. When the preliminaries were over, the two mothers got down to business.

'How many guests may we invite from our side, Joyce?' Julia asked.

'I thought thirty, the same as we've put on the list from our side. That's in addition to you and Jerome's sister, of course.'

Felicity was sitting on the arm of her father's chair, swinging a foot from side to side.

'Thirty! Is that all? I've got hordes of

friends who'll want to come and see old Jerry getting hitched!'

'Are they all friends of his as well?' Joyce enquired. She had gathered from her daughter that Felicity could be a bit difficult, and she had come prepared to stand firm.

'Not particularly,' Felicity drawled, her eyes cold.

'Then I'm afraid it won't be possible to invite them all. Perhaps one or two?'

'Huh! In that case you may find them crashing the party anyway.'

'That's enough, Fliss!' Quentin Marshall spoke up quietly. 'We must abide by Mrs Clarke's decision in this case.'

'It'll be a pretty shabby wedding, then,' she mumbled, but she knew better than to argue with him. As Jerome had explained to Mickey, his father was an easy-going chap until he was pushed too far, but when that happened the sparks would fly.

Mickey realised that she'd been holding her breath while this exchange was going on, but now the crisis seemed to be over. The talk moved on to other things.

When they were sitting round the fire, enjoying toasted teacakes, the subject of Tom Bowman came up.

'I assume he's still safely behind bars?' Quentin asked.

'Yes, indeed,' Joyce nodded. 'They let my husband visit him this week, and I can tell you that young man is feeling very sorry for himself indeed.'

'Sorry he's been caught, no doubt!'

Joyce didn't feel it was the time or the place to relay the message Tom had sent to Mickey. In fact, she didn't think her daughter needed to hear it at all.

'He was blubbering like a baby,' Joe Clarke had said in disgust. 'He kept saying it was Mickey he really loved. The only reason he'd left her for Felicity was the large amount of money involved. He'd planned to return to Mickey later and try to pick up the pieces. Can you imagine! He mustn't care much about her if he was prepared to make her an accessory after the fact!'

Now Joyce chose her words carefully 'There's one good thing about all this, young Bowman told my husband that the bulk of the money is safely tucked away in the bank, under his alias, Todd Bowles.'

Felicity sat up straight. 'Does that mean I'll get my money back?'

'Apparently so, some of it at least.'

'Probably not for a while, though,' Jerome put in. 'I imagine there will be a lot of red tape to be unravelled and the money may be held as evidence until his case comes to trial. Then there's Lydia Frew to be considered. I'm not sure how the money will be divided up in the end. Do we know how much is still left?'

'Quite a bit, I imagine. He told Joe he wanted to lie low until all the fuss had died down. Did he give you any hint of having all that cash when he was with you, Mickey?'

'Not at all. He seemed to be like me, living from pay day to pay day. He didn't get much of a salary from the golf club. But as we now know, he'd defrauded Lydia before he even met me, so all the time we were together he must have had her money hidden away somewhere.'

'So apart from living expenses after he disappeared with Felicity's inheritance, and then his ticket to Australia, he probably hasn't squandered a great deal,' Julia Marshall suggested. 'Why did he go to Australia, by the way? It seems like a mad idea, considering the circumstances.'

'He told my husband that he'd heard so much about it from Mickey that he really fancied seeing the country. When he came into money — that was the way he put it — he decided it was as good a place as any to hide away in.

'Australia is a big country and he thought that as long as he stayed well away from Canberra there was no danger of his running into us. Of course, it was pure serendipity that I happened to be visiting Sydney and spotted him there.'

The next few weeks passed in a blur as there was so much to be done. Mickey had to work out her notice at the office, for Jerome had persuaded her not to continue on there after their wedding. 'It's not that I'm being a chauvinist or anything,' he explained, 'but because of my level of income, taxation would take away all your earnings, so you'd virtually be slaving away for nothing. If you don't want to be a stay-at-home wife, perhaps you could train for some other career and return to the work force later.'

But Mickey had a secret hope that some day in the not too distant future she would be involved in what she considered to be the most important career in the world. She smiled to herself at the thought of caring for rosy babies who looked like Jerome in miniature.

There were fittings to be endured for the bride and bridesmaid; no store carried the sort of gowns that Mickey had envisioned, but Joyce knew a talented dressmaker who was able to produce just what was wanted.

St Margaret's Church was booked for December the twenty-eighth, and rooms were secured in several local B & B establishments where out of town relatives would stay. It was fortunate that not only Mickey, but her mother as well had grown up in this town. Both had attended St Margaret's throughout their lives so the vicar was more than happy to accommodate them, even though the Christmas season was a busy one for him.

One of the B & B proprietors had been a babysitter for Mickey long ago, and was thrilled to be involved in this way. 'I was planning to go to see my sister at Cambridge right after Christmas,' she bubbled, 'but I wouldn't miss this for anything! I'll come and line up outside the church to see the bride coming out!'

'I'll bring you a piece of wedding

cake,' Mickey promised.

'You do that, and I'll put it under my pillow and dream of my future husband!' Bertha laughed. She had already survived two husbands and made no secret of the fact that she was looking around for a third!

'Where are you going to live when you're married?' Sandie wanted to know.

'We'll use Jerome's flat for a bit when we come back from Australia,' Mickey told her. 'That's while we're looking around for a house. It has to be somewhere in town, or nearby, because of his work. Don't worry, you won't be losing sight of me forever.'

'It won't be the same, though,' Sandie mourned. 'No more late nights watching videos in our pyjamas and eating popcorn.'

'You'll forget about that when Brendan pops the question!' Mickey teased.

Yes, life was moving on, and both girls had much to look forward to.

* * *

The great organ peeled out joyfully as the beautiful bride, dressed in winter white, came down the aisle of St Margaret's on her father's arm. Behind them came Sandie, resplendent in forest green velvet, beaming with every step she took.

Jerome Marshall waited at the altar, his eyes moist as he saw his bride approaching, but Sandie had eyes only for the best man who stood at his side.

The evening before, Brendan Powell had asked her to marry him, and she had accepted. It seemed that Mickey's hunch had been correct. According to him he had been in love with her for some time, but had been unable to pluck up the courage to ask her. Being invited to be part of the wedding party had brought him to the point.

Joe Clarke slid into the pew behind his wife, and they watched proudly as Mickey turned and handed her bouquet of red roses and white freesias to Sandie. The vicar cleared his throat and began the ceremony.

'Dearly beloved . . . '

Everything went according to plan, as all weddings should. As the couple pledged their vows to each other, Joyce Clarke and Julia Marshall sniffed happily into lace-edged handkerchiefs, and one of the great aunts sobbed audibly. Nobody paid any attention to Felicity, sulking in the front row. There was nothing she could do to spoil such a joyous day.

Because it was the end of December, permission had been obtained to take photos inside the church, with the magnificent stained glass windows as a backdrop. Joyce had decreed that standing shivering on the steps outside was not a good idea.

'We must have just one picture out there, though,' Mickey pleaded. 'I do want one of us leaving the church.'

Remarkably, when they stepped outside, the sun peeked out from behind the clouds, which everyone thought was a good omen. A spattering of applause came from the little crowd of people who had waited to see the newlyweds leaving the church.

'Happy the bride the sun shines on,' the elderly great aunt quoted, and Mickey smiled at this. Come rain or shine she knew she was going to be happy with Jerome. Oh, no doubt they would have their ups and downs, their glad times and sad times, but that was only to be expected. That was life, but she was determined to make their years together the best they could.

'Smile, please!' the photographer called.

The bride and groom beamed at each other and the camera clicked.

THE END